J. H. (Joseph Henry) Shorthouse

The Little Schoolmaster Mark

A Spiritual Romance

J. H. (Joseph Henry) Shorthouse

The Little Schoolmaster Mark
A Spiritual Romance

ISBN/EAN: 9783337007829

Printed in Europe, USA, Canada, Australia, Japan

Cover: Foto ©Andreas Hilbeck / pixelio.de

More available books at **www.hansebooks.com**

THE LITTLE
SCHOOLMASTER MARK

𝔄 𝔖piritual 𝔕omance

BY

J. H. SHORTHOUSE

AUTHOR OF 'JOHN INGLESANT'

𝔏ondon

MACMILLAN AND CO.

AND NEW YORK

1894

Part I—First Edition, October 1883. Reprinted December 1883
Part II—First Edition, 1884. Reprinted twice February 1885
Complete Edition made up from parts 1885. Reprinted 1891, 1894

Printed by R. & R. CLARK, Edinburgh.

PREFACE.

THE readers of German autobiography (and more delightful reading cannot be had) will perceive that I have made use of some passages in the childhood of Heinrich Jung-Stilling to create the character of Little Mark. The experience of the Princess as to private religious societies was also that of Stilling. Should this little tale induce any one, at present ignorant of Stilling's Autobiography, to read that book, they will forget any grudge they may have formed against the present writer. As a matter of common honesty I should wish to express the pleasure I have had in reading another delightful book, *Studies of the Eighteenth Century in Italy*, by Vernon Lee.

The words of the anthem in the concluding chapter are taken from a sermon by Canon Knox Little, "The Vision of the Truth," preached in St. Paul's in Lent 1883, and published in *The Witness of the Passion*. They are so exactly in accord with the message which the shadowy beings of my tale seem to have left me that I cannot force myself to coin another phrase.　　　J. H. S.

TO

Lady Alwyne Compton

BY PERMISSION

THIS VOLUME IS DEDICATED

THE

LITTLE SCHOOLMASTER MARK.

𝔄 𝔖𝔭𝔦𝔯𝔦𝔱𝔲𝔞𝔩 𝔚𝔬𝔪𝔞𝔫𝔠𝔢.

PART FIRST.

I.

THE Court Chaplain Eisenhart walked up
the village street towards the schoolhouse.
It was April, in the year 1750, and a soft
west wind was blowing up the street, across
the oak woods of the near forest. Between
the forest and the village lay a valley of
meadows, planted with thorn bushes and
old birch trees with snow-white stems :
the fresh green leaves trembled continually
in the restless wind. On the other side

B

of the street a lofty crag rose precipitously above a rushing mountain torrent. This rock is the spur of other lofty hills, planted with oak and beech trees, through the openings of which a boy may frequently be seen, driving an ox or gathering fire-wood on his half-trodden path. Here and there in the distance the smoke of charcoal-burners ascends into the sky. Between the street and the torrent stand the houses of the village, with high thatched roofs and walls of timber and of mud, and, at the back, projecting stages and steps above the rushing water. A paradise in the late spring, in summer, and in autumn, these wild and romantic woods, traversed only by a few forest paths, are terrible in winter, and the contrast is part of their charm. The schoolhouse stands in the upper part of the village, on the opposite side of the street to the rest of the houses, looking across the valley to the western sun. Two large birch trees are before the open door. The Court Chaplain pauses before he goes in.

How it comes to pass that a Court Chaplain should be walking up the street of this forest village we shall see anon.

At first sight there does not seem to be much schoolwork going on. A boy, or we should rather say a child, of fifteen is seated at an open window looking over the forest. He is fair-haired and blue-eyed; but it is the deep blue of an angel's, not the cold gray blue of a courtier's eyes. Around him are seated several children, both boys and girls; and, far from teaching, he appears to be relating stories to them.

The story, whatever it is, ceases as the Court Chaplain goes in, and both raconteur and audience rise.

"I have something to say to thee, schoolmaster," said the Chaplain, "send the children away. Thou wilt not teach them anything more to-day, I suspect."

The children went away lingeringly, not at all like children just let loose from school.

When they were gone the expression of the Chaplain's face changed—he looked at the little schoolmaster very kindly, and sat down on one of the benches, which were black and worn with age.

"Last year, little one," he said, "when the Herr Rector took thee away from the Latin school and from thy father's tailoring, and confirmed thee, and thou tookest thy

first communion, and he made thee schoolmaster here, many wise people shook their
heads.   I do not think," he continued, with
a smile, "that they have ceased shaking
them when they have seen in how strange
a manner thou keepest school."

"Ah, your Reverence," said the boy,
eagerly, "the good people are satisfied
enough when they see that their children
learn without receiving much correction;
and many of them even take pleasure in
the beautiful tales which I relate to the
children, and which they repeat to them.
Every morning, as soon as the children
enter the school, I pray with them, and
catechise them in the principles of our
holy religion, as God teaches me, for I use
no book.   Then I set the children to read
and to write, and promise them these

charming tales if they learn well. It is impossible to express with what zeal the children learn. When they are perverse or not diligent I do not relate my histories, but I read to myself."

"Well, little one," said the Court Chaplain, "it is a strange system of education, but I am far from saying that it is a bad one. Nevertheless it will not last. The Herr Rector has his eye upon thee, and will send thee back to thy tailoring very soon."

The tears came into the little schoolmaster's eyes, and he turned very pale.

"Well, do not be sad," said the Chaplain. "I have been thinking and working for thee. Thou hast heard of the Prince, though thou hast, I think, never seen the pleasure palace, Joyeuse, though it is so near."

"I have seen the iron gates with the golden scrolls," said the boy. "They are like the heavenly Jerusalem; every several gate is one pearl."

The Chaplain did not notice the confused metaphor of this description.

"Well," he said, "I have been speaking to the Prince of thee. Thou knowest nothing of these things, but the Prince has lived for many years in Italy, a country where they do nothing but sing and dance. He has come back, as thou knowest, and has married a wife, according to the traditions of his race. Since he came back to Germany he has taken a fancy to this forest-lodge, for at first it was little more, and has garnished it and enlarged it according to his southern fancies; that is why he likes it better than his princely cities.   He has two children—a boy and a girl—eight and nine, or thereabouts.   The Princess is not a good woman.   She neglects her children, and she prefers the princely cities to her husband, to her little ones, and to the beautiful forests and hills."

The little schoolmaster listened with open eyes.   Then he said, beneath his breath :

" How Satanic that must be !"

" The Prince," continued the Court Chaplain, "is a beautiful soul 'manqué,' which means spoilt.   His sister, the Princess Isoline von Isenberg-Wertheim, *is* such a soul.   She has joined herself to a company of pious people who have taken an old manor-house belonging to the Prince on the farther side of the palace gardens, where they devote themselves to prayer, to good

works, and to the manufacture of half-silk
stuffs, by which they maintain themselves
and give to the poor.   The Prince himself
knows something of such feelings.   He
indeed knows the way of piety, though he
does not follow it.   He acknowledges the
grace of refinement which piety gives, even
to the most highly bred.   He is particularly desirous that his children should
possess this supreme touch.   Something
that I told him of thee pleased his fancy.
Thy strange way of keeping school seemed
to him very new ; more especially was he
delighted with that infancy story of thee
and old Father Stalher.   The old man,
I told the Prince, came into thy father's
for his new coat and found thee reading.
Reading, in any one, seemed to Father
Stalher little short of miraculous ; but

in a child of eight it was more—it was elfish.

"'What are you doing there, child?' said Father Stalher.

"'I am reading.'

"'Canst thou read already?'

"'That is a foolish question, for I am a human being,' said the child, and began to read with ease, proper emphasis, and due distinction.

"Stalher was amazed, and said:

"'The devil fetch me, I have never seen the like in all my life.'

"Then little Mark jumped up and looked timidly and carefully round the room. When he saw that the devil did not come, he went down on his knees in the middle of the floor and said:

"'O God! how gracious art thou.'

"Then, standing up boldly before old Stalher, he said :

"' Man, hast thou ever seen Satan ?'

"' No.'

"' Then call upon him no more.'

" And the child went quietly into another room.

"And I told the Prince what thy old grandfather used to say to me.

"' The lad is soaring away from us; we must pray that God will guide him by His good Spirit.'

"When I told all this to the Prince, he said :

"' I will have this boy.   He shall teach my children as he does the village ones. None can teach children as can such a child as this.'"

The little schoolmaster had been look-

ing before him all the time the Chaplain
had been speaking, as though in something of a maze. He evidently saw
nothing to wonder at in the story of himself and old Stalher. It seemed to him
commonplace and obvious enough.

"I shall send up a tailor from Joyeuse
to-morrow," said the Chaplain; "a court
tailor, such as thou never saw'st, nor thy
father either. He must measure thee for
a court-suit of black. Then we will go
together, and I will present thee to the
Prince."

II.

A FEW days after this conversation there was a melancholy procession down the village street. The Court Chaplain and the schoolmaster walked first; the boy was crying bitterly. Then followed all the children of the school, all weeping, and many peasant women, and two or three old men. The Rector stood in a corner of the churchyard under a great walnut tree and looked on. He did not weep. The Court Chaplain looked ashamed, for all the people took this misfortune to be of his causing.

When they had' gone some way out

of the village the children stopped, and, collecting into a little crowd, they wept more than ever. The Chaplain turned round and waved his hand, but the little schoolmaster was too troubled to take any farewell. He covered his face with his hands and went on, weeping bitterly. At last they passed away out of sight.

When they had gone on some distance, the boy became calmer ; he took his hands from his face, and looked up at the Chaplain through his tears.

"What am I to do when I come to the Prince, your Reverence ?" he said.

"Thou must make a bow as best thou canst," said the other ; "thou must not speak till the Prince speaks to thee, and thou must say 'Highness' sometimes, but not too often."

"How am I to tell when to say 'Highness' and when to forbear?" said the boy.

"Ah! that I cannot tell thee. Thou must trust in God; He will show thee when to say 'Highness' and when not."

They went forward in this way across the meadows, and through the scattered forest for two leagues or more, in the midday heat. The boy was not used to labour, and he grew very tired and unhappy. It seemed to him that he was leaving behind all that was fair and true and beautiful, and going to that which was false and garish and unkind. At last they came to an open drive, or avenue of the forest, where great oaks were growing. Some distance up the avenue they saw a high park pale stretching away on either hand, and in the centre of the drive were iron gates covered with gilt scrolls and letters. The Court Chaplain pushed the gates open, and they went in.

Inside, the forest drive was planted with young trees in triple rows. After walking for some distance they reached another gate, similar to the first, but provided with " loges," or guardrooms, on either side. One or two soldiers were standing listlessly about, but they took no heed. Here the drive entered the palace gardens, laid out in grass plots and stone terraces, and crossed by lofty hedges which shut out the view. They approached the long façade of a house with pointed roofs and green shutter blinds to all the windows. Here the Chaplain left the path, and conducted his companion to a remote side entrance ; and, after passing through many

passages and small rooms, at last left him
to the tender mercies of the court tailor
and some domestics, at whose hands the
little schoolmaster suffered what appeared
to him to be unspeakable indignities. He
was washed from head to foot, his hair was
cut, curled, and frizzled, and he was finally
arrayed in a plain suit of black silk, with
silk stockings, and delicate shoes with
silver buckles, and plain linen bands like
a clergyman. The worn homespun suit
that had become dear to him was ruth-
lessly thrown upon a dust-heap, and a message was sent to Herr Chaplain that his
protégé was now fit to be presented to the
Prince.

The boy could scarcely restrain his
tears; he felt as though he were wandering through the paths of a miserable dream.

Ah! could he only awake and find himself again in the old schoolhouse, narrating the adventures of the Fair Melusina to the attentive little ones.

The Chaplain led him up some back stairs, and through corridors and ante-rooms, all full of wonderful things, which the boy passed bewildered, till they reached a small room where were two boys apparently of his own age. They appeared to have been just engaged in punching each other's heads, for their hair was disordered, their faces red, and one was in tears. They regarded the Chaplain with a sullen suspicion, and the schoolmaster with undisguised contempt. The door at the farther side of the room was partly open, the Chaplain scratched upon it, and, receiving some answer, they went in.

The little schoolmaster dared scarcely breathe when he got into the room, so surprising was all he saw. To the left of the door, as they came in, was placed a harpsichord, before which was standing, with her back towards them, a young girl whose face they could not see ; by her side, at the harpsichord, was seated an elderly man upon whom the boy gazed with wonder, so different was he from anything that he had ever seen before ; opposite to them, in the window, hung a canary in a cage, and the boy perceived, even in the surprise of the moment, that the bird was agitated and troubled. But the next moment all his attention was absorbed by the figure of the Prince, who was seated on a couch to the right of the room, and almost facing them. To say that this was the most wonderful sight that the little schoolmaster had ever seen would be to speak foolishly, for he had seen no wonderful sights, but it surpassed the wildest imagination of his dreams. The Prince was a very handsome man of about thirty-five, of a slight and delicate figure, and of foreign manners and pose. He was dressed in a suit of what seemed to the boy a wonderful white cloth, of a soft material, embroidered in silk, with flowers of the most lovely tints. The coat was sparingly ornamented in this manner, but the waistcoat, which was only partly seen, was a mass of these exquisite flowers. At his throat and wrists were masses of costly lace, and his hair was frizzled, and slightly powdered, which increased the delicate expression of his features, which were perfectly cut. He lay back on the couch, caressing, with his right hand, a small monkey, also gorgeously dressed, and armed with a toy sword, who sat on the arm of the sofa cracking nuts, and throwing the shells upon the carpet.

The Prince looked up as the two came in, and waved his disengaged hand for them to stand back, and the next moment the strange phantasmagoria, into which the boy's life was turned, took another phase, and he again lost all perception of what he had seen before; for there burst into the little room the most wonderful voice, which not only he and the Chaplain, but even the Maestro and the Prince, had well-nigh ever heard.

The girl, who was taking her music lesson, had been discovered in Italy by the old Maestro, who managed the music of the private theatre which the Prince had formed. He had heard her, a poor untaught girl, in a coffee-house in Venice, and she afterwards became, in the opinion of some, the most pathetic female actress and singer of the century.

The first chord of her voice penetrated into the boy's nature as nothing had ever done before ; he had never heard any singing save that of the peasants at church, and of the boys and girls who sang hymns round the cottage hearths in the winter nights.

The solemn tramp of the Lutheran measures, where the deep basses of the men drown the women's soft voices, and the shrill unshaded singing of the children, could hardly belong to this art, which he heard now for the first time. These sudden runs and trills, so fantastic and difficult, these chords and harmonies, so quaint and full of colour, were messages from a world of sound, as yet an unknown country to the boy. He stood gazing upon the singer with open mouth. The Prince moved his jewelled hand slightly in unison with the notes; the monkey, apparently rather scared, left off cracking his nuts, and, creeping close to his master, nestled against his beautiful coat close to the star upon his breast.

Then suddenly, in this world of wonders, a still more wonderful thing occurred. There entered into this bewitching, this entrancing voice, a strange, almost a discordant, note. Through the fantasied gaiety of the theme, to which the sustained whirr of the harpsichord was like the sigh of the wind through the long grass, there was perceptible a strain, a tremor of sadness, almost of sobs.   It was as if, in the midst of festival, some hidden grief, known beforetime of all, but forgotten or suppressed, should at once and in a moment well up in the hearts of all, turning the dance-measures into funeral chants, the love-songs into the loveliest of chorales. The Maestro faltered in his accompaniment; the Prince left off marking the time, he swept the monkey from him with a movement of his hand, and leaned forward eagerly in his seat : the discarded favourite slunk into a corner, where it leaned disconsolately against the wall.   The pathetic strain went on, growing more tremulous and more intense, when suddenly the singing stopped, the girl buried her face in her hands and sank upon the floor in a passion of tears; the boy sprang forward, he forgot where he was, he forgot the Prince—

"It is the bird," he cried, "the bird!"

The canary, whose dying struggles the singer had been watching through her song, gave a final shudder and fell lifeless from its perch.

The Prince rose: he lifted the singer from her knees, and, taking her hands from the wet face, he turned to the others with a smile.

"Ah, Herr Chaplain," he said, "you come in a good hour. This then is the angel-child. They will console each other."

And, picking up the monkey as he passed, he left the room by another door.

III.

WHEN the Prince was gone the Maestro gathered up some music and turned to his pupil, who was drying her eyes and looking somewhat curiously at the boy through her tears.

"Well, Signorina," he said, "you truly sang that very well. If you could bring some of that 'timbre' into your voice always, you would indeed be a singer. But you are too light, too 'frivole.' I wish we could have a canary always who would die;" and, bowing very slightly to the Chaplain, he left the room.

Then the Chaplain looked kindly at the young people.

"Fräulein," he said, "this is the young tutor to the little serene Highnesses, I will leave you together, as the Prince wished."

When they were alone the boy felt very uncomfortable. He was very shy. This perhaps was as well, for there was no shyness at all on the part of his companion.

"So," she said, looking at him with a smile, and eyes that were again bright, "you are the new toy. I have heard of you. You are a wonderful holy child; what they call 'pious' in this country. How very funny! come and give me a kiss."

"No, Fräulein," said Mark, blushing still more, "that would be improper in me."

"Would it?" said the girl lightly; "don't

angels kiss?   How very stupid it must be
to be an angel!   Come and look at poor
'Fifine' then!   I suppose she is quite
dead."

And, opening the cage, she took out
the piteous heap of yellow feathers and
held it in her delicate hand, while the tears
came again into her large dark eyes.

"Ah! it was dreadful," she said, "to
sing and see him die."

"But, Fräulein," said the boy, "you
sang most beautifully.   I never heard anything so wonderful.   It was heaven itself."

The girl looked at him very kindly.

"Oh, you like my singing," she said, " I
am glad of that.   Do you know, we shall
be great friends.   I like you.   You are a
very pretty boy."

And she tried to put her arm round his

neck. Mark eluded her embrace. "Fräulein," he said, with a dignified air, which made his companion laugh, "you must remember that I am tutor to their serene Highnesses; I shall be very glad to be friends with you, and you will tell me something about the people in the palace."

"Oh!" replied the girl, "there is no one but our own company, but they are the greatest fun, and better fun here than anywhere else. It is delightful to see them among these stupid, solemn, heavy Germans, with their terrible language. I shall love to see you with them, you will stare your pretty eyes out. There's old Carricchio—that's not his name, you know, but he is called so because of his part— that is the best of them, they are always the same—off the stage or on it—always laughing, always joking, always kicking up their heels. You will see the faces—such delicious grimaces, old Carricchio will make at you when he asks you for the salt. But don't be frightened, I'll take care of you. They are all in love with me, but I like you already better than all of them. You shall come on yourself sometime, just as you are ; you will make a delightful part."

Mark stared at her with amazement.

"But what are these people ?" he said ; "what do they do ?"

"Oh, you will see," she said, laughing ; "how can I tell you. You never dreamt of such things ; you will stare your eyes out. Well, there's the Prince, and the little Highnesses, and the old *Barotin*, the governess, and "—here a change came over the girl's face—"and the Princess is coming soon, I hear, with her '*servente.*'"

"The Princess!" said the boy, "does she ever come?"

"Yes, she comes, sometimes," said his companion. "I wish she didn't. She is a bad woman. I hate her"

"Why? and what is her '*servente?*'"

"I hate her," said the girl; "her *servente* is the Count—*Cavalière-servente,* you know"—and her face became quite hard and fierce—"he is the devil himself."

The little schoolmaster's face became quite pale.

"The devil!" he said, staring with his large blue eyes.

"Oh! you foolish boy!" she said, laughing again, "I don't mean that devil. The Count is a much more real devil than he!"

The boy looked so dreadfully shocked that she grew quite cheerful again.

"What a strange boy you are!" she said, laughing. "Do you think he will come and take you away? I'll take care of you—come and sit on my lap;" and, sitting down, she spread out her lap for him with an inviting gesture.

Mark rejected this attractive offer with disdain, and looked so unspeakably miserable and ready to cry that his companion took pity upon him.

"Poor boy," she said, "you shan't be teased any more. Come with me, I will take you to the *Barotin*, and present you to the little serene Highnesses. They are nice children—for Highnesses; you will get on well with them."

Taking the boy's unwilling hand, she

D

led him through several rooms, lined with old marquetterie cabinets in the Italian fashion, till she found a page, to whom she delivered Mark, telling him to take him to the Baroness, into whose presence she herself did not appear anxious to intrude, that he might be presented to his future pupils.

The page promised to obey, and, giving him a box on the ear to ensure attention, a familiarity which he took with the most cheerful and forgiving air, she left the room.

The moment she was gone the page made a rush at Mark, and, seizing him round the waist, lifted him from the ground and ran with him through two or three rooms, till he reached a door, where he deposited him upon his feet. Then throwing open the door, he announced suddenly,

" The Herr Tutor to the serene Highnesses !" and shut Mark into the room.

His breath taken away by this atrocious
attack upon his person and dignity, Mark
saw before him a stately, but not unkindly-
looking lady and two beautiful children, a
boy and girl, of about eight and nine years
of age. The lady rose, and, looking at
Mark with some curiosity, as well she
might, said:

" Your serene Highnesses, this is the
tutor whom the Prince, your father, has
provided for you. You will no doubt
profit greatly by his instructions."

The little girl came forward at once,
and gave Mark her hand, which, not knowing what to do with, he held for a moment
and then dropped.

" My papa has spoken of you," she

said. " He has told me that you are very good."

" I shall try to be good, Princess," said Mark, who by this time had recovered his breath.

The little girl seemed very much insulted. She drew herself up and flushed all over her face.

" You must not say *Princess* to me," she said, " that is what only the little Princes say. You must say, 'my most gracious and serene Highness,' whenever you speak to me."

This was too much. Mark blushed with anger.

" May God forgive me," he said, " if I do anything so foolish. I am here to teach thee and thy brother, and I will do it in my own way, or not at all."

The little Princess looked as if she were about to cry, then, apparently thinking better of it, she said, with a half sob, and dropping the stately *"you"*:

"Well, my papa says that thou art an angel. I suppose thou must do as thou wilt."

The little boy, meanwhile, had been staring at Mark with solemn eyes. He said nothing, but he came, finally, to the little schoolmaster and put his hand in his.

What more might have been said cannot be told, for at this moment the page appeared again, saying that dinner was served at the third table, and that the Herr Tutor was to dine there.

The Baroness seemed surprised at this.

"I should have supposed," she said,

" that he would have dined with the Chaplain at the second table."

" No," asserted the page boldly, "the Prince has ordered it."

When alone, the Prince seldom dined ostensibly in public; but often appeared masqued at the third table, which was that of the actors and singers. He had given no orders at all about Mark. The arrangement was entirely of the Signorina's making, who desired that he should dine with her. It was a bold stroke; and an hour afterwards, when the Court Chaplain discovered it, measures were taken to prevent its recurrence—at least for a time.

In whatever way this arrangement came to be made, however, the result was very advantageous to Mark. In the first place, it was not formidable. The company took little notice of him.   Signor Carricchio made grotesque faces at others, but not at him.   He sat quite safe and snug by the Signorina, and certainly stared with all his eyes, as she had said.   The long, dark, aquiline features of the men, the mobile play of humorous farce upon their faces, the constant chatter and sport—what could the German peasant boy do but stare? His friend taught him how to hold his knife and fork, and how to eat.   The Italians were very nice in their eating, and the boy picked up more in five minutes from the Signorina—he was very quick— than he would have done in weeks from the Chaplain.

He was so scared and frightened, and the girl was so kind to him, that his boy's heart went out to her.

"What shall I call you, Signorina?" he said, as dinner was over. "You are so good to me." He had already caught the Italian word.

"My name is Faustina Banti," she said, looking at him with her great eyes; "but you may call me 'Tina,' if you like. I had a little brother once who called me that. He died."

"You are so very kind to me, Tina," said the boy, "I am sure you must be very good."

She looked at him again, smiling.

IV.

THE next morning early Mark was sent for to the Prince. He was shown into the dressing-room, but the Prince was already dressed. He was seated in an easy-chair reading a small closely-printed sheet of paper, upon which the word "Wien" was conspicuous to the boy. The Prince bade the little schoolmaster be seated on a fauteuil near him, and looked so kindly that he felt quite at his ease.

"Well! little one," said the Prince, "how findest thou thyself? Hast thou found any friends yet in this place?"

"The Signorina has been very kind to me, Highness," said the boy.

"Ah!" said the Prince, smiling, "thou hast found that out already. That is not so bad. I thought you two would be friends. What has the Signorina told thee?"

"She has told me of the actors who are so clever and so strange. She says that they are all in love with her."

"That is not unlikely. And what else?"

"She has told me of the Princess and of her servente."

"Indeed!" said the Prince, with the slightest possible appearance of increased interest; "what does she say of the Princess?"

"She says that she is a bad woman, and that she hates her."

"Ah! the Signorina appears to have

formed opinions of her own, and to be able to express them.   What else?"

"She says that the servente is the devil himself!   But she does not mean the real devil.   She says that the servente is a much more real devil than he!   Is not that horrible, Highness?"

The Prince looked at Mark for two or three moments, with a kindly but strange far-reaching look, which struck the boy, though he did not in the least understand it.

"I did well, little one," he said at last, "when I sent for thee."

There was a pause.   The Prince seemed to have forgotten the presence of the boy, who already was sufficiently of a courtier to hold his tongue.

At last the Prince spoke.

"And the children," he said; "thou hast seen them?"

"Yes," said Mark, with a little shy smile, " I did badly there. I insulted the gracious Fräulein by calling her ' Princess,' which she said only the little Princes should do; and I told her I was come to teach her and her little brother, and that I should do it in my own way or not at all."

The Prince looked as though he feared that this unexpected amusement would be almost too delightful.

"Well, little one," he said, "thou hast begun well. Better than this none could have done. Only be careful that thou art not spoilt. Care nothing for what thou hearest here. Continue to hate and fear the devil; for, whether he be thy own devil or the servente, he is more powerful than thou. Say nothing but what He whom thou rightly callest God teaches thee to say. So all will be well. Better teacher than thou my daughter could not have. I would wish her to be pious, within reason ; not like her aunt, that would not be well. I should wish her to care for the poor. Nothing is so gracious in noble ladies as to care for the poor. When they cease to do this they lose tone at once. The French noblesse have done so. I should like her to visit the poor herself. It will have the best effect upon her nature; much better," continued the Prince with a half smile, and seemingly speaking to himself, " much better, I should imagine, than on the poor themselves. But what will you have ?—some one must suffer, and the final touch cannot be obtained without."

There was another pause. This aspect of the necessary suffering the poor had to undergo was so new to Mark that he required some time to grasp it. The visits of noble ladies to his village had not been so frequent as to cause the malign effects to be deeply felt.

*　　*　　*　　*　　*

Acting upon this advice so far as he understood it, Mark pursued the same system of education with the little High-nesses as he had followed with the village children ; that is, he set them to read such things as he was told they ought to learn, and encouraged them to do so by promising to relate his histories and tales if they were good.

It is surprising how much the same human nature remains after generations of different breeding and culture. It is true that these princely children had heard many tales before, perhaps the very ones the little schoolmaster now related, yet they delighted in nothing so much as hearing them again. Much of this pleasure, no doubt, was due to the intense faith and interest in them shown by Mark himself. He talked to them also much about God and the unseen world of angels, and of the wicked one; and, as they believed firmly that he was an angel, they listened to these things with the more ready belief. Indeed, the affection which the little boy formed for his child-tutor was unusual. He was a silent, solemn child; he said nothing, but he attached himself to Mark with a persistent devotion.

Every one in the palace, indeed, took to

the boy: the pages left off teasing him; the
Signorina petted him in a manner sufficient
to deprive her numerous lovers of their
reason; the servants waited on him for
love and not for reward; but the strangest
thing of all was, that in proportion as he
was kindly treated—just as much as every
one seemed to love him and delight in
him—just so much did the boy become
miserable and unhappy. The kinder
these people were, the more he felt
the abyss which lay between his soul
and theirs; earnestness and solemn faith
in his—sarcasm and lively farce, and, at
the most, kindly toleration of belief, in
theirs.

Had they ill-treated or wronged him,
he would not have felt it so much; but
kindness and security on their part, seemed

to intensify the sense of doubt and per-
plexity on his.

It is difficult to realise the effect which
sarcasm and irony have upon such natures
as his. They look upon life with such a
single eye. It is so beautiful and solemn
to them. Truth is so true ; they are so
much in earnest that they cannot understand the complex feeling that finds relief
in sarcasm and allegory, that tolerates
the frivolous and the vain, as an ironic
reading of the lesson of life.

The actors were particularly kind to
him, though their grotesque attempts to
amuse him mostly added to his misery.
They were extremely anxious that he
should appear upon the stage, and indeed
the boy's beauty and simplicity would have
made an excellent foil.

E

"Herr Tutor," said old Carricchio the
arlecchino to him one day, with mock
gravity, " we are about to perform a comedy
—what is called a masqued comedy, not
because we wear masques, for we don't,
but because of our dresses. It consists of
music, dancing, love-making, joking, and
buffoonery; you will see what a trifle it is
all about. The scene is in the garden of
a country-house—during what in Italy we
call the Villeggiatura, that is the month we
spend in the country during the vintage.
A lady's fan is found by an ill-natured person in a curious place ; all the rest agree
not to see the fan, not to acknowledge that
it is a fan. It is all left to us at the moment, all except the songs and the music,
and you know how delightful those are.
If you would take a part, and keep your

own character throughout, it would be magnificent ; but we will wait, if you once see it you will wish to act."

No one, indeed, was kinder to Mark, or seemed more to delight in his society than the old arlecchino, and the two made a most curious sight, seated together on one of the terraces on a sunny afternoon. Nothing could be more diverse in appearance than this strangely assorted pair. Carricchio was tall, with long limbs, and large aquiline features. He wore a set smile upon his large expressive mouth, which seemed born of no sense of enjoyment, but of an infinite insight, and of a mocking friendliness. He seldom wore anything but the dress of his part ; but he wrapped himself mostly in a long cloak, lined with fur, for even the northern sunshine seemed chilly to

the old clown. Wrapped in this ancient
garment, he would sit beside Mark, listening
to the boy's stories with his deep un-
fathomed smile ; and as he went on with
his histories, the boy used to look into his
companion's face, wondering at the slow
smile, and at the deep wrinkles of the worn
visage, till at length, fascinated at the sight,
he forgot his stories, and looking into the
old man's face appeared to Mark, though
the comparison seems preposterous, like
gazing at the fated story of the mystic
tracings of the star-lit skies.

Why the old man listened so patiently
to these childish stories no one could tell ;
perhaps he did not hear them. He himself
said that the presence of Mark had the
effect of music upon his jaded and worn
sense. But, indeed, there was beneath

Carricchio's mechanical buffoonery and farce a sober and pathetic humour, which was almost unconscious, and which was now, probably owing to advancing years, first becoming known either to himself or others.

"The Maestro has been talking to me this morning," he said one day. "He says that life is a wretched masque, a miserable apology for existence by the side of art; what do you say to that?"

"I do not know what it means," said Mark; "I neither know life nor art, how can I tell?"

"That is true, but you know more than you think. The Maestro means that life is imperfect, struggling, a failure, ugly most often; art is perfect, complete, beautiful, and full of force and power. But I tell him that some failure is better than success; sometimes ugliness is a finer thing than beauty; and that the best art is that which only reproduces life.   If life were fashioned after the most perfect art you would never be able to cry, nor to make me cry, as you do over your beautiful tales."

Mark tried to understand this, but failed, and was therefore silent.   Indeed it is not certain whether Carricchio himself understood what he was saying.

He seemed to have some suspicion of this, for he did not go on talking, but was silent for some time.   These silences were common between the two.

At last he said:

" I think where the Maestro is wrong is in making the two quarrel.   They cannot quarrel.   There is no art without life, and

no life without art.   Look at a puppet-play
—the fantoccini—it means life and it means
art."

"I never saw a puppet-play," said Mark.

"Well, you have seen us," said Carricchio ; "we are much the same.   We move
ourselves—they are moved by wires ; but
we do just the same things—we are life and
we are art, in the burletta we are both.
I often think which is which—which is the
imposture and which is the masque.   Then
I think that somewhere there must be a
higher art that surpasses the realism of
life—a divine art which is not life but
fashions life.

"When I look at you, little one," Carricchio went on, "I feel almost as I do
when the violins break in upon the jar and
fret of the wittiest dialogue.   Jest and

lively fancy—these are the sweets of life, no doubt—and humorous thought and speech and gesture—but they are not this divine art, they are not rest. They shrivel and wither the brain. The whole being is parched, the heart is dry in this sultry, piercing light. But when the stringed melodies steal in, and when the rippling, surging arpeggios and crescendos sweep in upon the sense, and the stilled cadences that lull and soothe—then, indeed, it is like moisture and the gracious dew. It is like sleep; the strained nerves relax; the over-wrought frame, which is like dry garden mould, is softened, and the flowers spring up again."

Carricchio paused; but as Mark said nothing, he went on again.

"The other life is gay, lively, bright,

full of excitement and interest, of tender pity even, and of love—but this is rest and peace. The other is human life, but what is this? Art? Ah! but a divine art. Here is no struggle, no selfish desire, no striving, no conflict of love or of hate. It is like silence, the most unselfish thing there is. I have, indeed, sometimes thought that music must be the silence of heaven."

"The silence of heaven!" said Mark, with open eyes. "The silence of heaven! What, then, are its words?"

"Ah! that," said the old clown, smiling, but with a sad slowness in his speech, "is beyond me to tell. I can hear its silence, but not its voice."

V.

THE private theatre in the palace was a room of very moderate size, for the audience was necessarily very small; in fact, the stage was larger than the auditorium. The play took place in the afternoon, and there was no artificial light; many of the operatic performances in Italy, indeed, took place in the open air.

Yet, though the time of day and the natural light deprived the theatre of much of the strangeness and glamour with which it is usually associated, and which so much impress a youth who sees it for the first time, the effect of the first performance upon Mark was very remarkable. He was seated immediately behind the Prince. Far from being delighted with the play, he was overpowered as it went on by an intense melancholy horror. When the violins, the flutes, and the fifes began the overture, a new sense seemed given to him, which was not pleasure but the intensest dread. If the singing of the Signorina had been a shock to him, accustomed as he was only to the solemn singing of his childhood, what must this elfish, weird, melodious music have seemed, full of gay and careless life, and of artless unconscious airs which yet were miracles of art? He sat, terrified at these delicious sounds, as though this world of music without thought or conscience were a wicked thing. The shrill notes of

the fifes, the long tremulous vibration of
the strings, seemed to draw his heart after
them. Wherever this wizard call might
lead him it seemed he would have to follow
the alluring chords.

But when the acting began his terror
became more intense. The grotesque
figures seemed to him those of devils, or
at the best of fantastic imps or gnomes.
He could understand nothing of the dialogue, but the gestures, the laughter, the
wild singing, were shocking to him. When
the Signorina appeared, the strange intensity of her colour, the brilliancy of her eyes,
and what seemed to him the freedom of
her gestures and the boldness of her bewitching glances, far from delighting, as
they seemed to do all the others, made
him ready to weep with shame and grief.

He sank back in his seat to avoid the notice of the Prince, who, indeed, was too much absorbed in the music and the acting to remember him.

The beauty of the music only added to his despair; had it been less lovely, had the acting not forced now and then a glance of admiring wonder or struck a note of high-toned touching pathos even, it would not all have seemed so much the work of evil. When the comedy was over he crept silently away to his room; and in the excitement of congratulation and praise, as actors and audience mingled together, and the Signorina was receiving the commendations of the Prince, he was not missed.

He could not stay in this place—that at least was clear to him. He must escape. He must return to nature, to the woods

and birds, to children and to children's
sports. These gibing grimaces, these end-
less bowings and scrapings and false com-
pliments, known of all to be false, would
choke him if he stayed. He must escape
from the house of frivolity into the soft,
gracious outer air of sincerity and truth.

He cried himself to sleep : all through
the night, amid fitful slumber, the crowd
of masques jostled and mocked at him ;
the weird strains of unknown instruments
reached his half-conscious bewildered sense.
Early in the morning he awoke. There
had been rain in the night, and the smiling
morning beckoned him out.

He stole down some back stairs, and
found a door which opened on gardens and
walks at the back of the palace. This he
managed to open, and went out.

The path on which the door opened led him through rows of fruit-trees and young plantations. A little forest of delicate boughs and young leaves lifted itself up against the blue sky, and a myriad drops sparkled in the morning sun. The fresh cool air, the blue sky, the singing of the birds, restored Mark to himself. He seemed to see again the possibility of escape from evil, and the hope of right-eousness and peace. His whole spirit went out in prayer and love to the Almighty, who had made these lovely things. He felt as he had been wont to do when, on a fine Sunday, he had walked home with his children in order, relating to them the most beautiful tales of God. He wandered slowly down the narrow paths. The fresh-turned earth between the rows of saplings,

the beds of herbs, the moist grass, gave
forth a scent at once delicate and searching.
The boy's cheerfulness began to return.
The past seemed to fade.   He almost
thought himself the little schoolmaster
again.

After wandering for some time through
this delicious land of perfume, of light, and
sweet sound, he came to a very long but
narrow avenue of old elm trees that led
down a gradual slope, as it seemed, into
the heart of the forest.   Beneath the
avenue a well-kept path seemed to point
with a guiding hand.

He followed the path for some distance,
and had just perceived what seemed to be
an old manor-house, standing in a court-
yard at the farther end, when he was
conscious of a figure advancing along the

F

path to meet him : as it approached he saw that it was that of a lady of tall and commanding appearance, and apparently of great beauty ; she wore the dress of some sisterhood. When he was near enough to see her face he found that it was indeed beautiful, with an expression of the purest sincerity and benevolence. The lady stopped and spoke to Mark at once.

"You must be the new tutor to their Highnesses," she said ; " I have heard of you."

Mark said that he was.

"You do not look well," said the lady, very kindly ; " are you happy at the palace."

"Are you the Princess Isoline ?" said Mark, not answering the question ; " I think you must be, you are so beautiful."

"I am the Princess Isoline," said the lady; "walk a little way with me."

Mark turned with the lady and walked back towards the palace. After a moment or two he said: "I am not happy at Joyeuse, I am very miserable, I want to run away."

"What makes you so unhappy? Are they not kind to you? The Prince is very kind, and the children are good children —I have always thought."

"They are all very kind, too kind to me," said the boy. "I cannot make you understand why I am so miserable, I cannot tell myself—the Prince is worse than all——"

"Why is the Prince the worst of all?" said the lady, in a very gentle voice.

"All the rest I know are wrong,"

replied the boy, passionately—"the actors, the Signorina, the pages, and all; but when the Prince looks at me with his quiet smile—when the look comes into his eyes as though he could see through time even into eternity—when he looks at me in his kindly, pitying way — I begin to doubt. Oh, Highness, it is terrible to doubt! Do you think that the Prince is right ?

The Princess was silent for a moment or two ; it was not that she did not understand the boy, for she understood him very well.

" No, I think you are right and not the Prince," she said at length, in her quiet voice.

There was a pause : neither seemed to know what to say next. They had now nearly reached the end of the avenue next the palace; the Princess stopped.

"Come back with me," she said, "I will show you my house."

They walked slowly along the narrow pathway towards the old house at the farther end. The Princess was evidently considering what to say.

' "Why do you know that they are all wrong?" she said at last.

"Highness," said the boy after a pause, "I have never lived amongst, or seen anything, since I was born, but what was natural and real—the forest, the fruit-trees in blossom, the gardens, and the flowers. I have never heard anything except of God—of the wretchedness of sin—of beautiful stories of good people. My grandfather, when he was alive, used to talk to me, as I sat with him at his char-coal-burning in the forest, of my forefathers who were all honest and pious people. There are not many Princes who can say that."

The Princess did not seem to notice this last uncourtly speech.

" ' I shall then find all my forefathers in Heaven,' I would say to him," continued Mark. " ' Yes, that thou wilt! we shall then be of high nobility. Do not lose this privilege.' If I lose this privilege, how sad that will be! But here, in the palace, they think nothing of these things—instead of hymns they sing the strangest, wildest songs, so strange and beautiful that I fear and tremble at them as if the sounds were wicked sounds."

So talking, the Princess and the boy went

on through the lovely wood ; at last they left the avenue and passed into the court-yard of a stately but decayed house. The walls of the courtyard were overgrown with ivy, and trees were growing up against the house and shading some of the windows. The Princess passed on without speaking, and entered the hall by an open door. As they entered, Mark could hear the sound of looms, and inside were several men and women at different machines employed in weaving cloth. The Princess spoke to several, and leading Mark onward she ascended a wide staircase, and reached at last a long gallery at the back of the house. Here were many looms, and girls and men employed in weaving. The long range of lofty windows faced the north, and over the nearer woods could be seen the vast sweep of the great Thuringian Forest, where Martin Luther had lived and walked. The risen sun was gilding the distant woods. A sense of indescribable loveliness and peace seemed to Mark to pervade the place.

"How happy you must be here, gracious Highness!" he exclaimed.

They were standing apart in one of the windows towards the end of the long room, and the noise of the looms made a continuous murmur that prevented their voices being heard by the others who were near.

The Princess looked at Mark for some moments without reply.

"I must speak the truth always," she said at last, "but more than ever to such as thou art. I am not happy."

The boy looked at her as though his heart would break.

"Not happy," he said in a low voice, "and you so good."

"The good are not happy," said the Princess, "and the happy are not good."

There was a pause; then the Princess went on:

"The people who are with me are good, but they are not happy. They have left the world and its pleasures, but they regret them; they live in the perpetual consciousness of this self-denial—this fancy that they are serving God better than others are; they are in danger of becoming jealous and hypocritical. I warn you never to join a particular society which proposes, as its object, to serve God better than others. You are safer, more in the way of serving God in the palace, even amid the singing and the music which seems to you so wicked. They are happy; they are thoughtless, gay, like the birds. They have at least no dark gloomy thoughts of God, even if they have no thoughts of Him at all. They may be won to Him, nay, they may be nearer to Him now than some who think themselves so good. Since I began this way of life I have heard of many such societies, which have crumbled into the dust with derision, and are remembered only with reproach.

Mark stood gazing at the distant forest without seeing it. He did not know what to think.

" I do not know why I have told you this," said the Princess; " I had no thought of saying such words when I brought you here. I seem to have spoken them without willing it. Perhaps it was the will of God."

"Why do you go on with this life," said Mark sadly, "if it be not good? The Prince would be glad if you would come back to the palace. He has told me so."

It seemed to the boy that life grew more and more sad. It seemed that, baffled and turned back at every turn, there was no reality, no sincere walk anywhere possible. The worse seemed everywhere the better, the children of this world everywhere wiser than the children of light.

"I cannot go back now," said the Princess. "When you are gone I shall forget this; I shall think otherwise. There is something in your look that has made me speak like this."

"Then are these people really not happy?" said Mark again.

"Why should they be happy?" said the Princess, with some bitterness in her voice. "They have given up all that makes life pleasant—fine clothes, delicate food, cunning harmonies, love, gay devices, and sports. Why should they be happy? They have dull work, none to amuse or enliven the long days."

"I was very happy in my village outside the palace gates," said Mark quietly; "I had none of these things; I only taught the little peasants, yet I was happy. From morning to night the path was straight before me, — a bright and easy path; and the end was always light. Now all is difficult and strange. Since I passed through the gates with the golden scrolls, which I thought were like the heavenly Jerusalem, all goes crooked and awry; nothing seems plain and righteous as in the pleasant old days. I have come into an enchanted palace, the air of which I cannot breathe and live; I must go back."

"No, not so," said the Princess, "you are wanted here. Where you were you were of little good. There were at least others who could do your work. Here none can do it but you. They never saw any one like you before. They know it and speak of it. All are changed some-what since you came; you might, it is true, come to me, but I should not wish it. The air of this house would be worse for you even than that of the palace which you fear so much. Besides, the Prince would not be pleased with me."

Mark looked sadly before him for some moments before he said :

" Even if it be true what you say, still I must go. It is killing me. I wish to do right and good to all ; but what good shall I do if it takes all my strength and life ? I shall ask the Prince to let me go back."

" No," said the Princess, " not that— never that. It is impossible, you cannot go back !"

" Cannot go back !" cried Mark. " Why ? The Prince is very kind. He will not keep me here to die."

" Yes, the Prince is very kind, but he cannot do that ; what is passed can never happen again. It is the children's phrase,

'Do it again.' It can never be done again.
You have passed, as you say, the golden
gates into an enchanted world ; you have
known good and evil ; you have tasted of
the fruit of the so-called Tree of Life ;
you cannot go back to the village.   Think."

Mark was silent for a longer space this
time.   His eyes were dim, but he seemed
to see afar off.

"No," he said at last, "it is true, I
cannot go back.   The village, and the
school, and the children have passed away.
I should not find them there, as they were
before.   If I cannot come to you, there is
nothing for me but to die."

"The Pagans," said the Princess, "the
old Pagans, that knew their gods but dimly,
used to say — " The God-beloved die
young."   It has been said since by Chris-

tian men.—Do not be afraid to die. Instead of your form and voice there will be remembrance and remorse; instead of indifference and sarcasm there will be contrition; in place of thoughtless kindliness a tender love. Do not be afraid to die. The charm is working now; it will increase when sight is changed for memory, and the changeful irritation of time for changeless recollection and regret. The body of the sown grain is transfigured into the flower of a spiritual life, and from the dust is raised a mystic presence which can never fade. Do not be afraid to die."

Mark walked slowly back to the palace. He could not think; he was stunned and bewildered. He wished the Princess Isoline would have let him come to

her.   Then he thought all might yet
be well.   When he reached the palace
he found everything in confusion.   The
Princess and her friend the *servente* had
suddenly arrived.

LATER on in the day Mark was told that
the Princess wished to see him, and that
he must wait upon her in her own apartment. He was taken to a part of the
palace into which he had hitherto never
been ; in which a luxurious suite of rooms
was reserved for the Princess when she
condescended to occupy them. The most
easterly of the suite was a morning sitting-
room, which opened upon a balcony or
trellised verandah, shaded with jasmine.
The room was furnished in a very different
style from the rest of the palace. The

other rooms, though rich, were rather bare of garniture, after the Italian manner— their ornaments consisting of cabinets of inlaid wood and pictures on the walls, with the centre of the room left clear. These rooms on the contrary, were full of small gilt furniture, after the fashion of the French court. Curious screens, depicting strange birds of gaudy plumage, embarrassed Mark as he entered the room.

The Prince was seated near a lady who was reclining in the window, and opposite to them was a stranger whom Mark knew must be the Count. The lady was beautiful, but with a kind of beauty strange to the boy, and her dress was more wonderful than any he had yet seen, though it was a mere morning robe. She looked curiously at him as he entered the room.

" This, then," she said, " is the clown who is to educate my children."

At this not very encouraging address the boy stopped, and stood silently contemplating the group.

The Count was the first who came to his assistance.

" The youth is not so bad, Princess," he said. " He has an air of society about him, in spite of his youth."

The Prince looked at the Count with a pleased expression.

" Do not fear for the children, Adelaide," he said ; " they will fare very well. Their manners are improved already. When they come to Vienna you will see how fine their breeding will be thought to be. Leave them to me. You do not care for them ; leave them to me and to the Herr Tutor."

Mark was looking at the Count. This was another strange study for the boy. He was older than the Prince—a man of about forty; more firmly built, and with well-cut but massive features. He wore a peruke of very short, curled hair; his dress was rich, but very simple; and his whole appearance and manner suggested curiously that of a man who carried no more weight than he could possibly help, who encumbered himself with nothing that he could throw aside, who offered in every action, speech, and gesture the least possible resistance to the atmosphere, moral, social, or physical, in which he found himself. His manner to the Prince was deferential, without being marked, and he evidently wished to propitiate him.

"Thou art very pious, I hear," said the

Princess, addressing Mark in a tone of unmitigated contempt.

The boy only bowed.

" Is he dumb ?" said the Princess, still with undisguised disdain.

" No," said the Prince quietly. " He can speak when he thinks that what he says will be well received."

" He is wise," said the Count.

" Well," said the Princess sharply, "my wishes count for nothing ; of that we are well aware. But I do not want my children to be infected with the superstitions of the past, which still linger among the coarse and ignorant peasantry. I suppose, now, this peasant schoolmaster believes in a God and a hell, and in a heaven for such as he ?" and she threw herself back with a light laugh.

"No, surely," said the Count blandly, "that were too gross, even for a peasant priest."

"Tell me, Herr Tutor," said the Princess ; and now she threw a nameless charm into her manner as she addressed the boy, from whom she wished an answer ; "tell me, dost thou believe in a heaven ?"

"Yes, gracious Highness," said Mark.

"It has always struck me," said the Prince, with a philosophic air, "that we might leave the poor their distant heaven. Its existence cannot injure us. I have sometimes fancied that they might retort upon me : 'You have everything here that life can wish : we have nothing. You have dainty food, and fine clothes, and learning, and music, and all the fruition that your fastidious fancy craves : we are cold and hungry, and ignorant and miserable. Leave us our heaven! At least, if you do not believe in it, keep silence before us. Our belief does not trouble you; it takes nothing from the least of your pleasures; it is all we have.'"

"When the Prince begins to preach," said the Princess, with scarcely less contempt than she had shown for Mark, "I always leave the room."

The Count immediately rose and opened a small door leading to a boudoir. The Prince rose and bowed. The Princess swept to the ground before him in an elaborate curtsey, and, looking contemptuously, yet with a certain amused interest, at Mark, left the room.

The Prince resumed his seat, and, leaning back, looked from one to the other of his companions. He was really thinking with amusement what a so strangely - assorted couple might be likely to say to each other; but the Count, misled by his desire to please the Prince, misunderstood him. He supposed that he wished that the conversation which the Princess had interrupted should be continued, and, sitting down, he began again.

" I suppose, Herr Tutor," he said, "you propose to train your pupils so that they shall be best fitted to mingle with the world in which they will be called upon to play an important part ?"

The Prince motioned to Mark to sit, which he did, upon the edge of an embroidered couch.

" If the serene Highness," he said, " had wished for one to teach his children

who knew the great world and the cities
he would not have sent for me."

"What do you teach them, then?"

"I tell them beautiful histories," said
Mark, "of good people, and of love, and
of God."

"It has been proved," said the Count,
"that there is no God."

"Then there is still love," said the boy.

"Yes, there is still love," said the Count,
with an amused glance at the Prince; "all
the more that we have got rid of a cruel
God."

The boy's face flushed.

"How can you dare say that?" he said.

"Why," said the Count, with a simu-
lated warmth, "what is the God of you
pious people but a cruel God? He who
condemns the weak and the ignorant—the

weak whom He has Himself made weak,
and the ignorant whom He keeps in darkness—to an eternity of torture for a trivial
and temporary, if not an unconscious, fault?
What is that God but cruel who will not
forgive till He has gratified His revenge
upon His own Son? What is that God
but cruel—— But I need not go on. The
whole thing is nothing but a figment and a
dream, hatched in the diseased fancies of
half-starved monks dying by inches in caves
and deserts, terrified by the ghastly visions
of a ruined body and a disordered mind—
men so stupid and so wicked that they
could not discern the nature of the man
whom they professed to take for their God
—a man, apparently, one of those rare
natures, in advance of their time, whom
friends and enemies alike misconceive and

thwart; and who die, as He died, helpless and defeated, with a despairing cry to a heedless or visionary God in whom they have believed in vain."

As the Count went on, a new and terrible phase of experience was passing through Mark's mind. As the brain consists of two parts, so the mind seems dual also. Thought seems at different times to consist of different phases, each of which can only see itself—of a faith that can see no doubt—of a doubt that can conceive of no certainty; one week exalted to the highest heaven, the next plunged into the lowest hell. For the first time in his life this latter phase was passing through Mark's mind. What had always looked to him as certain as the hills and fields, seemed, on a sudden, shrunken and vanished away.

His mind felt emptied and vacant; he could not even think of God. It appeared even marvellous to him that anything could have filled this vast fathomless void, much less such a lovely and populous world as that which now seemed vanished as a morning mist. He tried to rouse his energies, to grasp at and to recover his accustomed thoughts, but he seemed fascinated; the eyes of the Count rested on him, as he thought, with an evil glance. He turned faint.

But the Prince came to his aid. He was looking across at the Count with a sort of lazy dislike; as one looks at a stuffed reptile or at a foul but caged bird.

"Thou art soon put down, little one," he said, with his kindly, lofty air. "Tell him all this is nothing to thee! That disease

and distraction never created anything.
That nothing lives without a germ of life.
Tell the Count that thou art not careful to
answer him—that it may be as he says.
Tell him that even were it so—that He of
whom he speaks died broken-hearted in
that despairing cry to the Father who
He thought had deserted Him—tell the
Count thou art still with Him! Tell him
that if His mission was misconceived and
perverted, it was because His spirit and
method was Divine! Tell the Count that
in spite of failure and despair, nay, per-
chance—who knows?—because even of
that despair, He has drawn all men to
Him from that cross of His as He said.
Tell the Count that He has ascended to
His Father and to thy Father, and, alone
among the personalities of the world's

story, sits at the right hand of God! Tell
him this, he will have nothing to reply."

And, as if to render reply impossible,
the Prince rose and, calling to his spaniel,
who came at his gesture from the sunshine
in the window, he struck a small Indian
gong upon the table, and the pages drawing back the curtains of the ante-chamber,
he left the room.

The Count looked at the boy with a
smile. Mark's face was flushed, his eyes
sparkling and full of tears.

"Well, Herr Tutor," said the Count
not unkindly, "dost thou say all that?"

"Yes," said the boy, "God helping me,
I say all that!"

"Thou might'st do worse, Tutor," said
the Count, "than follow the Prince."

And he too left the room.

VII.

THE arrival of the Princess very much increased the gaiety and activity of life within the palace. Every one became impressed with the idea that the one thing necessary was to entertain her. The actors set to work to prepare new plays, new spectacles ; the musicians to compose new combinations of quaint notes ; the poets new sonnets on strange and, if possible, new conceits. As the Princess was very difficult to please, and as it was almost · impossible to conceive anything which appeared new to her jaded intellect, the difficulty of the task caused any idea that promised novelty to be seized upon with a desperate determination. The most favourite one still continued to be the proposition that Mark should be induced, by fair means or foul, to take a part upon the 'stage. His own character—the *rôle* which he instinctively played—was so absolutely original and fresh that the universal opinion was confident of the success of such a performance.

" By some means or other," said old Carricchio, " he must be got to act."

" You may do what you will with him," said the Signorina sadly; " he will die. He is too good to live. Like my little brother and the poor canary, he will die."

In pursuit, then, of this ingenious plan, the Princess was requested to honour with her presence a performance of a hitherto unknown character, to be given in the palace gardens. She at first declined, saying that she had seen everything that could be performed so often that she was sick of such things, and that each of their vaunted and promised novelties proved more stale and dull than its precursor. It was therefore necessary to let her know something of what was proposed; and no sooner did she understand that Mark was to be the centre round which the play turned, than she entered into the plot with the greatest zeal.

It is, perhaps, not strange that to such a woman Mark's character and personality offered a singular novelty and even charm. The thought of triumphing over this child-like innocence, of contrasting it with the licence and riot which the play would offer, struck her jaded curiosity with a sense of delicious freshness, and she took an eager delight in the arrangement and contrivance of the scenes.

In expansion of the idea suggested by some of the wonderful theatres in Italy, where the open-air stage extended into real avenues and thickets, it was decided that the entire play should be represented in the palace gardens: and that, in fact, the audience should take part in the action of the drama. This, where the whole household was theatrical, and where the actors were trained in the Italian comedy, which left so much to the *improvisatore*— to the individual taste and skill of the actor—was a scheme not difficult to realise.

The palace garden, which was very

large, was disposed in terraces and hedges; it was planted with numerous thickets and groves, and, wherever the inequalities of the ground allowed it, with lofty banks of thick shrubs crowned with young trees, beneath which were arranged statues and fountains in the Italian manner. The hedges were cut into arcades and arches, giving free access to the retired lawns and shady nooks; and these arcades, and the lofty groves and terraces, gave a constant sense of mystery and expectation to the scene. The ample lawns and open spaces afforded more than one suitable stage, upon which the most important scenes of a play might be performed.

Beneath one of the highest and most important banks, which stretched in a perfectly straight line across the garden, planted thickly with flowering shrubs and fringed at the top with a long line of young trees, whose delicate foliage was distinct against the sky, was placed the largest of the fountains. It was copied from that in the Piazza Santa Maria in Transtevere in Rome, and was ornamented with great shells, fish, and Tritons. On either side of the fountain, and leading to the terrace at the back, were flights of marble steps, with wide-stretching stone bases upon either side towering above the grass. In front of the fountain and of the steps, beyond a belt of greensward, were long hedges planted in parallel rows, and connected in arches and arcades, crossing and re-crossing each other in an intricate maze, so that a large company, wandering through their paths, might suddenly appear and disappear. Beyond the hedges the lawn stretched out again, broken by flowerbeds and statues, and fringed by masses of foliage and lofty limes. A sound of falling water was heard on all sides ; and, by mysterious contrivance of concealed mechanism, flute and harp music sounded from the depths of the bosky groves.

Mark knew little of what was going on. He occupied himself mostly with his young pupils ; but the conversation he had had with the Princess Isoline had troubled his mind, and a sense of per-plexity and of approaching evil weighed upon his spirits and affected his health. He, who had never known sickness in his peasant life, now, when confined to a life so unnatural and artificial, so out of harmony with his mind and soul, became listless and weak in body, and haunted by fitful terrors and failings of consciousness. He knew that some extraordinary preparations were being made ; but he was not spoken to upon the subject, and paid little attention to what was going on. Indeed, had he been in the least of a suspicious nature, the entire absence of solicitation or interference might have led him to suspect some secret machination against his simplicity and peace, some contrived treachery at work ; but no such idea crossed his mind, he occupied himself with his own melancholy thoughts and with the histories and parables which he related to his pupils.

On the morning of the day fixed for the performance, then, things being in this condition, Mark rose early. He had been informed that it was necessary that he should wear his best court-suit, which we have seen was of black silk with white bands and ruffles. He gave his pupils a short lesson, but their thoughts were so much occupied by the expectation of the coming festivity that he soon released them and wandered out into the gardens alone. The performance of the play had been fixed for noon.

The day was bright and serene. The gardens were brilliant with colour and sweet with the perfume of flowers and herbs. Strains of mysterious harmony from secret music startled the wanderer along the paths.

Mark strayed listlessly through the more distant groves. He was distressed and dissatisfied with himself. His spirit seemed to have lost its happy elasticity, his mind its active joyousness. The things which formerly delighted him no longer seemed to please, even the loveliness of nature was unable to arouse him. He found himself envying those others who took so much real delight, or seemed to him to do so, in fantastic and frivolous music and jest and comic sport. He began to wonder what this new surprising play—these elaborately prepared harmonies—these swells and runs and shakes—might prove to be. Then he hated himself for this envy—for this curiosity. He wished to return to his old innocence—his old simplicity.

But he felt that this could never be. As the Princess had told him, whatever in after years he might become, never would he taste this delight of his child's nature again. He was inexpressibly sad and depressed.

As he wandered on, not knowing where he went, and growing almost stupid, and indifferent even to pain, he found himself suddenly surrounded by a throng of dancing and laughing girls. It was easy, in this magic garden, to steal unobserved upon any one amid the bosky hedges and arcades; but to surprise one so abstracted as the dreamy and listless boy required no effort at all. With hands clasped and mocking laughter they surrounded the unhappy Mark. They were masqued, with delicate bits of fringed silk across the eyes, but had they not been so he was too confused to have recognised them. He tried in vain to escape. Then he was lifted from the ground by a score of hands and borne rapidly away.

The stories of swan-maidens and winged

fairies of his old histories crossed his mind, and he seemed to be flying through the air; suddenly this strange flight came to an end; he was on his feet again, and, as he looked confusedly around, he found that he was alone.

He was standing on a circular space of lawn, surrounded by the lofty wood. In the centre was an antique statue of a faun playing upon a flute. He seemed to recognise the scene, but could not in his confusion recall in what part of the vast garden it lay.

As he stood, lost in wonder and expectation, a fairy-like figure was suddenly present before him, from whence coming he could not tell. The slim and delicate form was dressed in a gossamer robe, through which the lovely limbs might be seen. She held a light masque in her hand, and laughed at him with her dancing eyes and rosy mouth. It was the little Princess, his pupil.

Even now no thought of plot or treachery entered the boy's mind; he gazed at her in wondering amaze.

"You must come with me," said the girl-princess, holding out her hand; " I am sent to fetch you to the under world."

Behind them as they stood, and facing the statue of the faun, was a cave or hollow in the wood, half concealed by the pendant tendrils of creeping and flowering plants. It seemed the opening of a subterranean passage. The child pushed aside the hanging blossoms and drew Mark, still dazed and unresisting, after her. They went down into the dark cave.

*   *   *   *   *

Meanwhile from early dawn the palace had been noisy with pattering feet. For its bizarre population was augmented from many sources, and the great performance of the day taxed the exertions of all. As the morning advanced visitors began to arrive, and were marshalled to certain parts of the gardens where positions were allotted them, and refreshments served in tents. They were mostly masqued. Then strange groups began to form themselves before the garden front of the palace, and on the terraces. These were all masqued, and dressed in variety of incongruous and fantastic costumes, for though the play was supposed to be classical, yet the necessity of entertaining the Princess with something

startling and lively was more exacting than
artistic congruity. As we have seen, the
Prince had always inclined more to the fairy
and masqued comedy than to the serious
opera, and on this occasion the result was
more original and fantastic than had ever
before been achieved.

As the morning went on, there gradually
arranged itself, as if by fortuitous incident,
as strange a medley of fairy mediæval legend
and of classic lore as eye ever looked upon.
As the Prince and Princess, surrounded by
their principal guests, all masqued and
attired in every shade of colour and diver-
sity of form, stood upon the steps before
the palace, the wide gardens seemed full of
groups equally varied and equally brilliant
with their own. From behind the green
screens of the hedges, and from beneath

the arcades, figures were constantly emerg-
ing and passing again out of sight,
apparently accidentally, but in fact with a
carefully-devised plan. Strains of delicate
music filled the air.

Then a group of girls in misty drapery,
and masqued across the eyes, the same
indeed that had carried off Mark, appeared
suddenly before the princely group. They
had discovered in the deepest dell of their
native mountain a deserted babe — the
offspring doubtless of the loves of some
wandering god. They were become its
nurses, and fed it upon sacred honey and
consecrated bread. Of immortal birth
themselves, and untouched by the passing
years, the boy became, as he grew up, the
plaything, and finally the beloved of his
beautiful friends. But the boy himself is

indifferent to their attractions, and careless or averse to their caresses. He is often lost to them, and wanders in the mountain fastnesses with the fawns and kids.

All this and more was told in action, in song, and recitative, upon the palace lawns before this strange audience, themselves partly actors in the pastoral drama. Rural dances, and games and sacrifices were presented with delicately-conceived grouping and pictorial effect. Then the main action of the drama developed itself. The most lovely of the nymphs, the queen and leader of the rest, inspires a devoted passion in the heart of the priest of Apollo, before whose altar they offer sacrifice, and listen for guiding and response. She rejects his love with cruel contempt, pining always for the coy and errant boy-god, who thinks of

I

nothing but the distant mountain summits and the divine whispers of the rustling woods. The priest, insulted and enraged, invokes the aid of his divinity, and a change comes over the gay and magic scene. A terrible pestilence strikes down the inhabitants of these sylvan lawns, and gloomy funerals, and the pathetic strains of dirges take the place of dances and lively songs.

The terrified people throw themselves before the altar of the incensed Apollo, and the god speaks again. His anger can be appeased only by the sacrifice of the contemptuous nymph who has insulted his priest, or of some one who is willing to perish in her place. Proclamation is made across the sunny lawns, inviting a victim who will earn the wreath of self-sacrifice and of immortal consciousness of a great deed, but there is no response.

The fatal day draws on ; the altar of sacrifice is prepared ; but there spreads a rumour among the crowd—fanned probably by hope—that at the last moment a god will interfere. Some even speak of the wandering boy, if he could only be found. Surely he—so removed from earthly and selfish loves, so strange in his simplicity, in his purity—surely he would lay down his guileless life without a pang. Could he only be found! or would he appear!

The herald's voice had died away for the third time amid a fanfare of trumpets. At the foot of the steps of the long terrace, by the Roman fountain, a delicate and lovely form stood on the grassy verge before the altar, by the leaping and rushing

water's side; a little to the left, whence the
road from Hades was supposed to come,
stood the divine messenger, the lofty
herald—clad in white, with a white wand;
behind the altar stood the wretched priest,
on whom the fearful task devolved, the
passion of terror, of pity, and of love, traced
upon his face; all sound of music had died
away; a hush as of death itself fell upon
the expectant crowd; from green arch and
trellised walk the throng of masques, actors
and spectators alike, pressed forward upon
the lawn before the altar. . . . The priest
tore the fillet from his brow and threw
down his knife.

*   *   *   *   *

The darkness of the cave gave place to
a burst of dazzling sunlight as Mark and
the little Princess, who in the darkness

had resumed her masque, came out suddenly from the unseen opening upon one of the great stone bases by the side of the steps. To the boy's wonderstruck sense the flaring light, the mystic and awful forms, the thronged masques, the shock of surprise and terror, fell with a stunning force. He uttered a sharp cry like that of a snared and harmless creature of the woods. He pressed his hands before his face to shut out the bewildering scene, and, stepping suddenly backward in his surprise, fell from the edge of the stone platform some eight feet to the ground. A cry of natural terror broke from the victim, in place of the death-song she was expected to utter, and she left her place and sprang forward towards the steps. The crowd of masques which surrounded the Prince came forward tumultuously, and a hurried movement and cry ran through the people, half of whom were uncertain whether the settled order of the play was interrupted or not.

Mark lay quite still on the grass, his eyes closed, the Signorina bending over him ; but the herald, who was in fact director of the play, waved his wand imperiously before the masques, and they fell back.

"Resume your place, Signorina," he said, "this part of the play has, apparently, failed. You will sing your death-song, and the priest will offer himself in your stead."

But the girl rose, and, forcing her way to where the Prince stood, threw herself upon his arm.

"Oh, stop it, Highness, stop it!" she

cried, amid a passion of sobs; "he is dying, do you not see!"

The Prince removed his masque; those around him, following the signal, also unmasqued, and the play was stopped.

PART SECOND.

I.

THERE was no change in the bright sunlight or in the festive colours of the gay
crowd. The grass was as green, the sky
as blue, the rushing leaping water sparkled
as before, nevertheless a sudden change
and deadness fell upon the garden and its
throng of guests. The hush that had preceded Mark's appearance was of a far
different kind. That had been a silence

K

of awe, of expectation, of excitement, and
of life ; this was the scared silence of dismay. Those who were most distant from
the Prince, and who could do so with
decency, began to scatter like frightened
children, and were lost in the arcaded
hedges and walks. The Prince remained
standing, his masque in his hand, the Signorina still weeping on his arm ; she was
too excited to admit of comfort, he stroked
her hand kindly, as he would that of a
child. The Herald, who was evidently
exceedingly disgusted at the turn things
had taken, and the quite unnecessary stop
that had been put to the play, had retired
a few paces, and was in conference with
Carricchio, who was apparently trying to
console him. The Princess, scared and
startled, was drawing the Count after her

to leave the scene, when a tall and beautiful woman emerged from a trellised walk and, through the respectful crowd that fell back to give her passage, advanced towards the Prince.

"You may resume your play, Ferdinand," she said, and her voice was very sad but without a touch of scorn; "you may resume your play. It is not you who have killed this child; it is I."

Then, stooping over the lifeless body, she raised it in her arms, and, in the midst of a yet more perfect stillness, as in the presence of a being of a holier and a loftier world, the Princess Isoline disappeared with her burden into the forest depths.

She followed the path under the narrow avenue, where she had once walked with Mark, till she reached her quiet and melancholy house; and, entering at once into the hall, she deposited her burden upon the long table, where the household was wont to dine. She laid it with the feet at one end of the board, and, straightening the stiffening limbs, she knelt down before it and buried her face in her hands.

"*The good are not happy, and the happy are not good*"—was she then good because she was so miserable? Ah no! Or was this wretchedness a wicked thing? Again, surely not!

As she lay thus, crushed and beaten down, her form contorted with sobs, a quiet footstep roused her, and, raising her eyes, she saw the Prince through her blinding tears. He was standing by the table, near the head of the child. His face was very pale, and the eyes had lost the habitual languor of their expression, and were full of an earnest tender grief. The Princess rose, and they looked each other straight in the eyes. Through the mist of tears the Prince's form became refined and purified, and he stood there with a beauty hitherto altogether unknown, even to her.

"I told this child, Isoline," he said; "I told this child that I had done well to send for him."

"Ferdinand," she said again, "it is not you who have done this; it is I." She stopped for a moment to recover control, and went on more passionately—"I, who pretended to the devoted life! in which alone he could breathe; I, to whom he looked for help and strength; I, who deserted him and gave a false report of the promised land."

The Prince looked at her with eyes full of compassion, but did not reply.

"You did what you could," continued his sister; "your effort was surely a noble one. More, in fact; you came to the help of his faith against evil. It is always so! The children of the world act always better than the children of light!"

In her self-abasement and despair the Princess did not remember Mark's words, that the greatest trial of his faith had been the Prince: a tolerance which is kindly and even appreciative, and yet, as with a clearness of a farther insight stands indifferently aside, must always be the great trial of simple faith.

"It is easier, Isoline," said her brother at last, "to maintain a low standard than a high. It seems to me that we have both

been wrong, but yours is the nobler fault.
You attempted an impossible flight—a
flight which human nature has no wings
strong enough to achieve. As for me,
this has been a terrible shock—more than
I could have thought possible, I who
fancied myself so secure and so serene.
That such a terrible chance could happen
shows how unstable are the most finished
schemes of life. I fancied that my life
was an art, and I dreamed that it might
be perfected—as a religious art. Fool
that I was! How can life or religion be
an art when the merest accident can dis-
solve the entire fabric at a blow? No art
can exist in the presence of an impalpable
mystery, of an unknown, inappeasable, im-
placable Force."

"No," said the Princess; "art is not

enough!—morality, virtue, love even, is not enough. None of these can pierce the veil. Nothing profits, save the Divine Humanity, which, through the mystery of Sacrifice, has entered the unseen. You know, Ferdinand," and she looked up through her tears with a sad smile, "in your art there was always in old times a mystery."

She rose as she said this, and stood more lovely than ever in her grief and in her faith ; and the Prince moved a step forward, and put his hand upon the breast of the child. As they stood, looking each other full in the eyes, in the notorious beauty of their order and of their race, it might have seemed to a sanguine fancy that, over the piteous victim of earth's failure, art and religion for the moment were at one.

II.

THE pleasure Palace was deserted. Mark was buried in a shadowy graveyard behind the old manor-house, where was a ruined chapel that had been a canonry. The Princess Isoline gave up her house, and dissolved her family. They were scattered to their several homes. She said that her place was by her brother's side. It would seem that none were sorry for some excuse. The Prince could no longer endure the place; he said that he had neglected his princely cities, and must visit them for a time. The Signorina was inconsolable, but her singing improved day by day. The Maestro began to have hopes of her. He wrote to Vienna concerning an engagement for her at the Imperial Theatre there, without even consulting the Prince, who for the moment was disgusted with the very name of art. Old Carricchio said that the northern sunshine was more intolerable than ever, and that he should return to Italy, but would take Vienna in his way. It might be supposed that this old man would have been much distressed, but, if this were the case, he concealed his feelings with his usual humorous eccentricity. He spent most of his time listening to Tina's singing. Even the Maestro and the pages seemed to miss Mark more.

In the general disorganisation and confusion the Princess even was not entirely unaffected. She was continually speaking of Mark, whose singular personality had struck her fancy, and whose sudden and pathetic death had touched her with pity. She appeared unusually affectionate to her husband and to his sister, and she despatched the Count to secure a residence in Vienna, where she expressed her intention of taking the entire family as soon as the Prince had satisfied his newly-awakened conscience by a sight of Wertheim. The children were delighted with the thought, and were apparently consoled for the absence of their tutor. Perhaps already his tales had begun to tire.

The Maestro and Carricchio were walking side by side upon the terrace where Mark was used to sit.

" I shall make a sensation at Vienna,"

said the Maestro; "that little girl is growing into an impassioned actress with a marvellous voice. I have an idea. I have already arranged the score. I shall throw this story into the form of opera—a serious opera, not one of your farcical things. It is a charming story, most pathetic, and will make people cry. That boy's character was exquisite: 'Ah,' they will say, 'that lovely child!'"

"I don't understand your pathos," said Carricchio crossly,—"the pathos of composers and writers and imaginative men. It is all ideal. You talk of farce, I prefer the jester's farce. I never knew any of you to weep over any real misery—any starving people, any loathsome, sordid poor!"

"I should think not," said the Maestro; "there is nothing delightful in real misery

—it is loathsome, as you say; it is horrible, it is disagreeable even! Art never contemplates the disagreeable; it would cease to be true art if it did. But when you are happy yourself, when you are surrounded by comfort and luxury—*then* to contemplate misery, sorrow, woe! Ah! this is the height of luxury: this is art! Yes, true art!"

"It seems selfish, to me," said the Arlecchino surlily.

"Selfish!" exclaimed the Maestro; "of course it is selfish! Unless it is selfish it cannot be art. Art has an end, an aim, an intention—if it deserts this aim it ceases to be art. It must be selfish."

There was a slight pause, then the Maestro, who seemed to be in great spirits, went on :

"I always thought the Prince a poor creature, now I am sure of it. He is neither one thing nor the other. He will never be an artist, in the true sense."

"He is very sorry for that poor child," said Carricchio.

"Sorry!" exclaimed the Maestro. "Sorry! I tell you when the canary died I was delighted, but I am still more delighted now. I predict to you a great future for the Signorina. She will be a great actress and singer. The death of this child is everything to us; it was just what was required to give her power, to stir the depths of her nature. *Mio caro*," he continued caressingly, putting his hand on Carricchio's arm, "believe me, *this* is life, and *this* is art!"

"He is a cold-blooded old devil," muttered Carricchio savagely, as he turned away, "with his infernal talk of art. I would not go to Vienna with him but for the Signorina. I will see her once upon the stage there. Then the old worn-out Arlecchino will go back into the sunshine, and die, and go to Mark."

III.

THE Maestro's romantic opera was a success. He was at least so far a genius that he knew where he was strong and where he was weak.

He reproduced with great exactness the play in the palace gardens, but he kept the person and character of Mark enshrouded in mystery, allowing him to appear very seldom, and trusting entirely to the singing of the principal performers, and especially of the Signorina, to impress the audience with the idea of his purity and innocence. He surpassed himself in the

L

intense wistful music of the score ; never
had he produced such pathetic airs, such
pleading sustained harmonies, such quiver-
ing lingering chords and cadences. At
the supreme moment the boy appears, and,
after singing with exquisite melody his
hapless yet heroic fate, offers his bosom to
the sacrificial knife. But a god intervenes.
Veiled in cloud and recognised in thunders,
a divine and merciful hand is laid upon
the child. Death comes to him as a sleep,
and over his dead and lovely form the
anger of heaven is appeased. Incapable
as the Maestro was of feeling much of the
pathos and beauty of his own work, still,
with that wonderful instinct, or art, or
genius, which supplies the place of feeling,
he produced, amid much that was grotesque and incongruous, a work of delicate

touch and thrilling and entrancing sound. The little theatre near the Kohl market, where the piece was first produced, was crowded nightly, and the narrow thoroughfares through private houses and court-yards, called Durch-häuser, with which the extraordinary and otherwise impenetrable maze of building which formed old Vienna was pierced through and through, were filled with fine and delicate ladies and gay courtiers seeking admission. So great, indeed, was the success that an arrangement was made with the conductors of the Imperial Theatre for the opera to be performed there. The Empress-Queen and her husband were present, the frigid silence of etiquette was broken more than once by applause, and the Abate Metastasio wrote some lines for the Signorina;

indeed, the success of the piece was caused by the girl's singing.

" Mark is better than the canary," the Maestro was continually repeating.

In his hour of triumph the old gentleman presented a quaint and attractive study to the observer of the by-ways of art. Amid the rococo surroundings among which he moved, he was himself a singular example of the power of art to extract from bizarre and unpromising material somewhat at least of pure and lasting fruit. He had attired his withered and lean figure in brilliant hues and the finest lace, and in this attire he trained the girl, also fantastically dressed, to warble the most touching and delicious plaints. The instinctive pathos of inanimate things, of forms and colours, was perceived in sound, and much that hitherto seemed paltry and frivolous was refined and ennobled. Mark's death, and even that of the poor canary, was beginning to bear fruit. Nature and love were feeling out the enigma of existence by the aid of art.

The reference to the canary was not, indeed, made in the presence of Tina, for the Maestro found that it was not acceptable. Nevertheless, a strange fellowship and affection was springing up between these two. The critics complained that the Signorina varied her notes; but, in fact, the score of the opera never remained the same—at least as regarded her parts. As she sang, with the Maestro beside her at the harpsichord, imagination and recollection, instructed by the magic of sound, touched her notes with an unconscious pathos and revealed to her master, with his ready pencil in one hand and the other on the keys, fresh heights and depths of cultured harmony, new combinations of fluttering, melodious notes.

This copartnership, this action and reaction, had something wonderful and charming about it; the power of nature in the girl's voice suggesting possibilities of more melodious, more artistic pathos to the composer, the girl's passionate instinct recognising the touch, and confessing the help, of the master's skill. It seems a strange duet, yet I do not know that we should think it strange.

The girl's nature, pure and loving, was supremely moved by the discovery of this power of realisation and expression which it had obtained; but at times it frightened her.

"I hate all this," she would cry some-times, starting away from the harpsichord; "they are dead and cold, and I sing!"

"Sing! *mia cara!*" the old man would say, with, for him, a soft and kindly tone; "you cannot help but sing : and when did love and sorrow feel so near and real to you as when, just now, you sang that phrase in F minor?"

"It is wicked!" said the girl ; but she sang over again, to the perfect satisfaction of her master, the phrase in F minor.

"It is true," she said, after a pause. "I knew not how to love—I knew not what love was till I learned to sing from you. Every day I learn more what love is ; I feel every hour more able to love— I love you more and more for teaching me the art of love."

"Ah, *mia cara*," said the Maestro, "that was not difficult! You were born with that gift. But it is strange to me, I confess it, how pathetically you sing. It is not in the music—at any rate, not in my music. It is beyond my art and even strange to it, but it touches even me."

And the old man shrugged his shoulders with an odd gesture, in which something like self-contempt struggled with an unaccustomed emotion.

The girl had turned half round, and was looking at him with her bright, yet wistful eyes.

"Never mind, Maestro," she said; "I shall love you always for your music, in spite of your contempt of love, and your miserable, cold——"

And she gave a little shudder. She

was forming, indeed, a passionate regard
for the old man, solely for the sake of his
art.

It was not by any means the first time
that such an event had occurred, for unselfish love is much more common than
cynical mankind believes.

IV.

THE Prince soon grew tired of Wertheim. Apart from other reasons, of which perhaps we may learn something hereafter, he felt lost without the accustomed *entourage* which he had attracted to Joyeuse. The death of Mark had made a profound impression upon his delicately strung temperament. It disturbed the lofty serenity of his life, it shocked his taste, it was bad art. That such a thing could have happened to him in the very citadel and arcanum of his carefully designed existence—and should have happened, too, as the result of his own individual purpose and action—arrested him as with an archangel's sword; showed him forcibly that his delicately woven mail was deficient in some important, but as yet unperceived, point; that his fancifully conceived prince-life was liable to sudden catastrophe. He had lived delicately, but the bitterness of death was not passed. He left Wertheim, and, travelling with his children and servants in several carriages and *chaises de poste*, he journeyed to Vienna, whither the Princess had preceded him.

The Prince travelled alone in a *carrosse-coupé*, or travelling chaise, at the head of his party. The Barotin and the children followed him in the second carriage, which was full of toys for their entertainment; now and again one or the other would be promoted for a stage or two to their father's carriage, to remain there as long as they entertained him. After a time they entered upon the flat plains of the Danube and approached Vienna.

As they crossed the flat waste of water meadows, over the long bridges of boats, and through the rows of poplars, a drive usually so dreary to travellers to Vienna, the sun broke out gloriously and the afternoon became very fine. For many miles before him, over the monotonous waste, the great tower of St. Stephen's Church had confronted the Prince, crowned with its gigantic eagle and surrounded by wheeling flocks of birds — cranes and ravens and daws. Herons and storks rose now and again from the ditches and pools by the wayside and flitted across the road. The brilliant light shone upon the mists of the river and upon the distant crags and woods.

The Prince was alone; the children were tired and restless from the long journey, and were sent back to the long-suffering Barotin. He lay back upon the rich furs which filled the carriage, and kept his eyes listlessly fixed upon the distant tower. The descending sun lighted up the weather-stains and the vari-coloured mosses that covered its sides; a rainbow, thrown across the black clouds of the north and east, spanned the heavens with a lofty arch.

The Prince gazed wearily over the striking scene. Existence appeared to him, at the moment, extremely compli-cated.

"It was a terrible mistake," he said, his thoughts still running on the old disaster; "a terrible mistake! Yet they cannot be right—Isoline and the people with her—who talk of nothing but sacrifice and self-denial, and denounce everything by which life is not only made endurable, but by which, indeed, it is actually maintained in being. What would life be if every one were as they? 'Ah!' she says, 'there is little chance of that! So few think of aught save self! So few deny themselves for the sake of others, you need not grudge us few our self-chosen path.' That is where they make the fatal mistake. Each man should carve out his life, as a whole, as though the lives of all were perfect, not as if it were a broken fragment of a fine statue; each should be a perfect Apollo of

the Belvedere Gardens, not a mere torso;
not a strong arm only that can strike, not
a finger only that can beckon—even though
it be to God. Because all cannot enjoy
them, does that make assorted colour, and
sweet sound, and delicate pottery less
perfect, less worthy to be sought? He
should aim at the complete life—should
love, and feel, and enjoy."

The great tower rose higher and higher
above the Prince as he thought these last
words aloud; the screaming kites and
daws wheeled above his head; the great
eagle loomed larger and larger in the
evening light. They passed over the
wide glacis, threaded the drawbridges and
barriers, and entered the tortuous narrow
streets. A golden haze lighted the
crowded thoroughfares and beautified the

carving and gables of the lofty houses. A motley crowd of people, from east and west alike, in strange variety of costume, thronged the causeways, and hardly escaped the carriage-wheels in their reckless course. The sight roused the Prince from his melancholy, and he gazed with an amused and even delighted air from his carriage-windows. His nature, pleasure-loving and imaginative, found this moving life a source of never-tiring interest and suggestiveness. The fate, the interests, the aims, and sorrows of every human figure that passed across his vision, even for a second, formed itself in some infinitely slight, yet perfectly real and tangible, degree in his mind; and he conceived the stir and tremor of a great city's life with a perfect grasp of all the little de-

M

tails that make up the dramatic, the graphic whole.

The carriage swept through the Place St. Michael, past the Imperial Palace, and, pursuing its course through the winding streets to the imminent peril of the populace of Croats, Servians, Germans, and a mixed people of no nation under heaven, reached the *Hôtel* which had been selected for the Prince in the Tein quarter.

Though this quiet quarter is in close neighbourhood to the most busy and noisy parts of the city, the contrast was striking. The Prince saw nothing here but quaint palaces crowded together within a space of a few hundred yards. Here were the palaces of the Lichtensteins, the Festetics, the Esterhazys, the Schönbornes. Antique escutcheons were hanging before the houses, and strange devices of the golden fleece, and other crests and bearings were erected on the gables and roofs. Vienna was emphatically the city of heraldry, and a tendency towards Oriental taste in noble and burgher produced a fantastic architecture of gables and minarets, breaking the massive lines of fortress-like mediæval palace and *hôtel*. Here and there a carriage was standing in the quiet street, and servants in gaudy liveries stood in the sunshine about the steps and gates.

The next morning the Prince was seated at his toilette, in the hands of his dresser, who was frizzling and powdering his hair. By his side was standing his valet or body-servant, as he would be called in England —*Chasseur* or *Jager*, as he was called in North or South Germany. This man was

one of the most competent of his order,
and devoted to his master.

"Well, Karl," the Prince was saying,
with his kindly air, "thou breathest again
here, I doubt not. This place is more to
thy mind than Joyeuse—*n'est ce pas?*
There is life here and intrigue. It is
better even than Rome? Is it so?"

"Wherever the Serene Highness is," replied Karl graciously, "I am content and
happy. I was happy in Rome, in Joyeuse,
at Wertheim; but I confess that I like
Wien. There is colour here, and quaint-
ness, and *esprit.*"

Karl had picked up many art terms with
the rest of the princely household.

"Ah! Wertheim!" said the Prince,
rather sadly as it seemed. "I like
Wertheim, ah! so much—for a day or two.

One is so great a man there. I know every one, and every one knows me. I feel almost like a beneficent Providence, and as though I had discovered the perfection of art in life. When I walk in the garden avenue after dinner, between the statues, and every one has right of audience and petition, and one old woman begs that her only son may be excused from military service, and another that her stall in the market may not be taken away; and one old man's house is burnt down, and he wants help to rebuild it, and another craves right of wood-gathering in the princely forests, and another begs that his son may be enrolled among the under-keepers and beaters of the game, with right of snaring a hare,—and all these things are so easy to grant, and seem to these poor folks so gracious, and like the gifts of heaven, that one thinks for the moment that this must be the perfection of life. But it palls, Karl; in a day or two it palls! The wants and sufferings of the poor are so much alike; they want variety, they are so deficient in shade, they are such poor art!" and the Prince sighed wearily.

"That is natural for the Serene Highness," said Karl, with a sympathising pity which was amusing; "that is natural to the Serene Highness, who does not see below the surface, and to whom all speak with bated breath. There is plenty of light and shade in the lives of the poor, if you go deep enough."

"Ah!" said the Prince with interest, "is it so? Doubtless now, within a few yards of us, there are art-scenes enacted, tragedies and comedies going on, of which you know the different *rôles*—one of which, maybe, you fill yourself. Eh, Karl?"

"It is a great city, Highness," said Karl. "They are all alike, good and ill, love and hatred, the knave and the fool. All the world over, it is much the same."

At this moment, the hair-powdering being over, the Prince rose.

"Well," he said, "to-night the Signorina sings at the Imperial Theatre. She and the Maestro sup with me afterwards. The Princess sups at the Palace."

V.

It is difficult at the present day to realise such scenes as that presented by the Imperial Theatre during the performance that evening. The comparative smallness of the interior and dimness of the lights, combined with the incomparable splendour and richness in the appearance of the audience which filled every portion of the theatre, even to the gallery of the servants, with undiminished brilliancy, produced an effect of subdued splendour and of a mystic glow of colour which we should look for in vain in any theatre in Europe now.

The Empress-Queen and her husband occupied a central box, and the Court, graduated according to rank, and radiating from this centre, filled boxes, pit, and gallery. The Prince's box was on the royal tier, not far from the Empress. He was accompanied by the Princess and his sister.

"I am delighted with Isoline," the Princess said; "that poor child's death has worked wonders upon her in a way no one would have expected. She seems to have thrown off her singular fancies, and behaves as other people do."

"Isoline never was very easy to understand," said the Prince.

Whether or not she were inspired by the presence of the Prince, the Signorina had never sung so wonderfully as she did that night. The frigid silence of Imperial etiquette, so discouraging and chilling to southern artists, gave place, now and again, to an irrepressible murmur of emotion and applause. The passionate yearning of the purest love, the pathos of unselfish grief, found a fit utterance in notes of an inimitable sweetness, and in melodies whose dainty phrases were ennobled and mellowed at once by delicate art and loftiest feeling. The house gave way at last to an uncontrollable enthusiasm, and, regardless of Court etiquette, the entire assembly rose to its feet amid a tumult of applause.

Not far from the Maestro, who was conducting the music from the centre of the orchestra, was seated Carricchio. He had, of course, discarded his professional

164 TIIE LITTLE SCHOOLMASTER MARK.

dress, and had attired himself, according to the genius of his countrymen, in rich but dark and plain attire. Any one who could have watched his face—that face which the little Schoolmaster was used to wonder at—and could have marked the quaint mingling, on the large worn features, of the old humorous movement with the new emotions of wonder and of love, would not have spent his moments in vain.

But the success was too complete. The Empress-Queen was shocked at the breach of decorum. She was not in the least touched by the Signorina's singing, and the story of the opera was unintelligible to her. It was suggested by those who were offended and injured by the success of the piece, and by the displacement of other

operas, that this arrangement entailed increased expense upon the royal treasury,
and, amid the penurious and pettifogging
instincts of the Court of Vienna in those
days, this was a fatal thrust.   The theatre,
it was said, was required for other pieces,
notably for a new opera by Metastasio
himself.

"It was very beautiful, Ferdinand,"
said the Princess, as they left the box;
and, struck by her tone and by the unaccustomed use of his name, the Prince
looked at her with surprise, for it was
years since he had seen the sweet, softened,
well-remembered look in her eyes. " I
liked that boy !"

" I will convey your approbation to the
Signorina," replied the Prince; "it will
complete the triumph of the night."

"Where do you sup to-night, Ferdinand?" said the Princess.

"I—I sup in private with the Maestro and Tina," said the Prince.

"Ah!" said the Princess, still with the same wistful, unaccustomed look. "There is a cover laid for me at the Imperial table —I must go."

It is absurd to talk of what would have happened had the threads of our lives been woven into different tissues, else we might say that but for that Imperial cover the issues of this story would have had a different close.

The Maestro waited at the theatre till the Signorina had changed her dress. When she appeared she was radiant with triumph and delight, but the old man was sad and depressed. Some intimation of the fatal resolution had been conveyed to him in the interval.

"What is the matter with you, Maestro?" said the girl; "you ought to be delighted, and you look as gloomy as a ghost. What is it?"

"It is nothing," said the Maestro. "I am an old man, *mia cara*, and the performance tires me. Let us go to the Prince."

They entered a fiacre, and were driven to the courtyard of the Prince's *Hôtel*.

The supper, though private, was luxurious, and was attended by all the servants of the Prince. Inspired by the success of the night, the Prince exerted himself to please; but, apart from all other circumstances, the Signorina would have delighted any man. She was at that delightful age when the girl is passing into the woman;

she was increasing daily in beauty, she
was perfectly dressed, she was radiant that
night with happiness, and with the consciousness of success ; she was touched by
the recollection of the past, and profoundly
affected by the power of expression which
she had found in song ; more than this—
much more—she was drawn irresistibly by
a feeling of pity and sympathy towards
the old man; she could not understand his
depression and gloom ; she paid little
attention to the Prince, but lavished a
thousand pretty arts and delicate attentions
on the vain endeavour to rouse her friend.
No other conduct could have rendered her
so attractive in the eyes of the Prince.
To his refined and really high-toned taste,
this pretty devotedness, this manifestly
pure affection and gratitude, as of a

daughter, commended by such loveliness and vivacity, were irresistible. It was exactly that combination of pathos and grace and art that suited his cultured fancy and the long habit of his trained life. He was inexpressibly delighted and happy. Forgetful of past mistake and misfortune, he congratulated himself on his success in attaching to his person and family so lively and dulcet a creature. His scheme of life seemed complete and authorised to his conscience by success.

Once more he uttered the fatal words, "*I will have* this girl."

"You are the happiest man I know, Maestro," he said; "you are truly a creative artist, for you not only create melodious sounds and spirit-stirring ideas, but you actually create flesh and blood

N

sirens and human creatures as lovely as
your sounds, and far more real. The
Signorina is your work, and see, as is
natural, how devoted she is to her maker."

"Every one thinks others happier than
himself, Prince," said the old man, still
gloomy. "As for the Signorina, she has
much more made me than I her. I shall
only injure and cripple her."

The girl looked at him with tears in
her eyes.

"The Maestro is not well," she said to
the Prince; "he will be more cheerful
to-morrow. Success frightens him. It is
often more terrible than failure."

"He fears that you will forsake him,
when you are courted and praised so
much," said the Prince in a low voice, for
the old man seemed scarcely to notice

what passed; "he fears you will forsake him," and as he spoke the Prince kept his eyes fixed inquiringly on the girl's face.

The Signorina said nothing. She turned her dark great eyes full on the old man, and the Prince wanted no more than what the eyes told him.

"She is a glorious creature," he said to himself.

VI.

THE next morning the crash came. The Maestro was informed that only one more performance could be allowed at the Imperial Theatre, and that, further, there were difficulties in the way of the performance being permitted in any theatre in Vienna. The old man was crushed: he came to the Signorina with the notice in his hand.

"*Mia cara,*" he said, making great efforts to be calm, "this is the end. I am a broken and a ruined man. I have been all my life waiting for this chance—this gift of inspiration. I thought that it would never come; it tarried so long, and I grew so old. At last it came, but only just in time. I have never written anything like this music, and never shall again. Now it is stopped. I must go. I cannot stay where it must not be played; I must go somewhere, and take my music with me. It will not be for long. The Prince will not leave Vienna. He is pleased with the city and with his reception. I must leave you all."

The girl was on her feet before him, with flashing eyes which were full of tears.

"Maestro!" she said; "what mean you to talk in this way? Do you suppose that I will ever leave you, that I will stay if you go? I owe everything to you. I cannot sing without you. I will follow

you to Paris—anywhere. Whatever fortune awaits you shall await us both."

"Ah, Tina," said the old man, "you
are very good, but you mistake. I am not
the great master you suppose. I know
it too well. There is always something
wanting in my notes. When you sing
them, well and good. Even as they are
they never would have been scored but
for you. When I leave you the glamour
will be taken out of them. They will be
cold and dead : no one will think anything
of them any more."

"If this be true," said the girl, almost
fiercely, "it is all the more reason why I
will never leave you! You have made
me, as the Prince said ; I am yours for
life. Wherever you go I will go ; whatever you write I will sing. If we fail, we

fail together. If we succeed, the success is yours."

She paused for a moment, and then, with a deeper flush and a tender confidence which seemed inspired :

"And we shall succeed! I have not yet sung my best. I, too, know it. You have not yet made me all you may. Whatever you teach me I will sing!"

The old man looked at her, as well he might, deeply moved, but he shook his head.

"Tina," he said, "I will not have it. You must not be ruined for me. You must not go. Other masters, greater than I, will finish what it is my happiness to have begun. The world will ring with your name. Art will be enriched with your glorious singing. I shall hear of it before I die. The old Maestro will say, 'Ah, that is the girl whom I taught.'"

The girl was standing now quite calm, all trace of emotion even had past away. She looked at him with a serene smile that was sublime in its rest. It was not worth while even to say a word.

*   *   *   *   *

The decision of the Maestro and the Signorina filled the princely household with distress. Tina had been, at Joyeuse, the light and joy of a joyful place; and, although the household saw much less of her at Vienna, yet the charm of her presence and of her triumphs was still their own. The Prince heard the news with absolute dismay. It was not only that he had begun to love the girl, he conceived that she belonged to him of right. The

Maestro was his; he had assisted, maintained, and patronised him; by his encouragement and in his service he had discovered the girl and trained her in music. They were both part of his scheme, of his art of life. It was bad, doubtless, that, when he had attempted still higher flights, when he had wished to bring, and, as he had once thought, succeeded in bringing, religion, faith, and piety, with all their delicate loveliness, to grace the abundance of his life's feast— it was bad, doubtless, that, at the moment of success, a terrible catastrophe should have cruelly broken this lovely plaything, and left him with a haunting conscience as of well-nigh a deliberate murderer. All this was bad, but now he seemed about to fail, not only in these original and high efforts, which perhaps had never been attempted before, but in the simplest schemes of art; and to fail, to be foiled by the perversity of a girl! He had great influence in Vienna; he doubted not but that he could soon overcome the opposition of interested rivals, or, if not exactly this, there were other masters besides this one, there was other music for the Signorina to sing. He believed with him that her future would be brilliant, and he considered himself the rightful possessor of her triumph and of her charm. He imperiously ordered the Maestro to remain.

The old man begged to be excused.

He was old and broken down, he said; he had taught the Signorina all he knew. Henceforward he must pass her on to abler teachers. It was no wish of his that she should accompany him, he had urged her to remain.

In truth, as was not wonderful, his whole heart was in this last music of his; as a matter of selfish pride and enjoyment even, apart from his narrow, though to some extent real, conceptions of art, he must hear it again performed in a great theatre, and that soon.

The vexation of the Prince became excessive. He lost his habitual ease and serenity of tone. He sent for Carricchio.

The Princess Isoline was with him.

"Let the girl go, Ferdinand," she was saying. "Let her go for a time. She will improve by travel, and by singing in other cities. She is of a grateful and affectionate nature; be sure that she will never forget you: she will return when you send for her."

Then, as Carricchio was announced, the Princess rose and left the room.

"Carricchio," said the Prince impetuously, "you must stop this nonsense of the Banti's leaving Vienna. If the Maestro chooses to stay, well and good. If he chooses to go, also good. He will be a stupid old fool! But it is his own business. I have nothing to do with it; but Tina shall not go. She belongs to me. I will not have it. You have influence with her, and must stop it."

"Highness," said Carricchio, "she will not go for long. The Maestro is old and broken; he will be helpless among strangers, hostile or indifferent. She will be friendless; she will be glad to come back ;" and there passed over Carricchio's face an unconscious habitual grimace.

"I tell you," said the Prince, "she shall not go at all. She belongs to me: voice and body and soul, she belongs to me."

He was flushed with excitement. In spite of the habitual dignity of manner and of gesture which he could not wholly lose, his appearance, as he stood in the centre of the room before Carricchio, was so strange, so different from its usual lofty quiet, that the latter looked at him with surprise, and even apprehension.

"*Mon Prince*," he said at last, "beware ! Take the warning of an old man. Let her alone. God warns every man once—sometimes twice—seldom a third time. My Prince, let her alone!"

"What, Carricchio !" said the Prince

lightly. "Are you also one of us? Are we all in love with a little singing-girl?"

"My Prince," said Carricchio, "it matters little what an old fool like me loves or does not love. I am a broken old Arlecchino, you a Prince. She will have none of us. She alone of all of us—Prince and Princess and clown alike—has solved the riddle which that boy, whom we killed, was sent to teach us. She alone has made her life an art, for she alone has found that art is capable of sacrifice. She alone of all of us has based her art upon nature and upon love. She is passionately devoted to her master—her father in art and life, for he rescued her from poverty and shame. She will follow him through the world. *Mon Prince*, let her alone."

"To let her go," said the Prince, "would

be to spoil everything. Shall I give up a deliberate plan of life, finely conceived and carefully carried out, to gratify the whims of a foolish girl? Why is religion to inter-fere always with art? Why is sacrifice always to be preached to us? Life is not sacrifice: it is a morbid, monkish idea. Life is success, fruition, enjoyment. Life is an art—religion also should be an art."

"Where there is love," said Carricchio, "there must be sacrifice, and no life is perfect without love. There are only two things capable of sacrifice—nature and love. When art is saturated with nature and elevated by love, it becomes a religion, but religion never becomes an art; for art without nature and without love is partial and selfish, and cannot include the whole of life. You will find, believe me, that if you follow art apart from these two, you have indeed only been following a deception, for it has not only been ir-religion, it has been bad art."

"The sphere of religion," said the Prince, "is the present, and its scope the whole of human life. It is, therefore, an art. If art is selfish, so is religion. The most disinterested martyr is selfish, for he is following the dictates of his higher self. I tell you Tina is mine, I want her. She shall not go!"

"You said the same of the boy, High-ness," said Carricchio gravely; "yet he went—went a long journey from us all *Mon Prince*, beware!"

VII.

FAILING with the old Arlecchino, the Prince determined to try his own influence with the girl; but he had no intention of acting in a blundering and inartistic manner. He was too good an artist not to prepare the way. Having failed with Carricchio, he resolved to try the Maestro once more.

He sent for the old man. "Maestro," he said, "I regret exceedingly what has happened. I do not wish to make a disturbance immediately after coming to Court after so long an absence. It would not be well. But we shall soon put things right.

Meanwhile, if you like to travel for a few months you can do so. There is no necessity for it that I know of, but it will be an entertainment for you, and you will gather ideas for your music, and, no doubt, fame also. If the Signorina remains here, you shall have letters of credit on Paris or any other city. As you will not be dependent on your music, it probably will be a great success. As the Scripture says, 'To him that hath shall be given.' When you are tired of wandering you can return. But Tina remains here — you understand."

"I have already tried to persuade her, Highness," said the old man.

"Well, you must try again. You shall sup with her to-night, as you are neither of you wanted at the opera. I will order supper for you in *la petite Salle* beyond the *salon*. When I return at night I shall find everything arranged."

The Prince himself went to the opera. He did not care to be seen, as he was supposed to have received a slight, but he had nothing else to do, and was interested in the performance, which was a new opera by Metastasio. Indeed, he was restless, and wanted diversion of any kind.

He sat well back in his box, across the front of which the delicate lace curtains were partly drawn. Karl the *Jager*, and the valet who attended, had left the box and retired to their own gallery, where they criticised the play and the music with more interest than did their master. The Prince lay back in his chair, watching the piece listlessly through the gauzy screen,

and listening half heedlessly to the music
—the wonderful music of Pergolesi.

The fairy world of song and harmony,
peopled by fantastic and impossible creatures who exist only for the sake of the
melodies which give them birth, was not
devoid of powerful and pathetic phases of
passion and of character ; but what made
its lesson particularly adapted to the
Prince's frame of mind, and gradually
aroused his languid interest, was the sub-
ordination of passion and character to the
nicest art. The deepest sorrow warbled
to exquisite airs ; passion, despairing and
bewildered, flinging itself as an evil thing
across the devious paths of Romance, yet
never for a second forgetful of the nicest
harmony or capable of a jarring note.
This ideal musical world — bizarre and

rococo as, in some respects, it was—seemed
to the Prince in some sort an allegory, or
even parody, on the art-life he had set himself to create or to perfect. He thought
he saw that even its faults were instinct
with, and revealed, the secret of which he
was in search. Faultiness and feebleness,
folly and littleness, seemed restrained, cor-
rected, transformed, when presented in
solemn, noble, and pure melodies. Everything in this parody of life was ruled by
art just as, in the so-called reality, he had
wished. The lesson was not altogether a
noble one. Passion, ennobled by art, lost
its fatal, repellent aspect, and became perfect as an artistic whole. Here the poison
worked readily in the Prince's mind. To
sacrifice the least portion of this art-life to
any narrow illiterate scruples was to sin

against its perfection, without which the whole structure were worthless. Better, far better, throw the entire scheme to the winds. Imperfect art is worse than none at all. He had already forgotten, if he had ever listened to it, Carricchio's warning against unreal and loveless art.

Moreover, as the play went on, and the fantastic adventures and fortunes of its strange actors gradually won the Prince's attention and attracted his interest, through the gauzy veil of the curtains and the haze of delicious melody, his desire was excited and he longed to play out his own part on a real stage, and with tangible, no longer ideal, delights and success. Why did he sit there gazing at a mere show of life, when life itself, in a form strangely attract-ive and prepared—life which he himself

had in some sort formed and created—
awaited him, with parts and scenes, ready
for the playing, compared to which all the
glamour of the piece before him was a mere
dream-shade ? Fortune had been kind to
him ; or rather, he thought, his patient
loyalty to art had wrought the usual result.
As he had followed his steadfast course,
nature, chance, the confusions and spite of
men, had all tended to co-operate with him,
had each supplied a thread of gold to perfect his brilliant woof of coloured existence.
The moment seemed at hand ; let him no
longer dally with shadows, but play his
own part, compared with which the piece
before him was poor and tame.

* * * * *

"*La petite Salle,*" as the Prince had
called it—in which supper had been laid

for Tina and the Maestro—was situated at the end of a splendid "*apartement*," which contained the *salon* and the other reception-rooms of the *Hôtel*. It communicated with other rooms and private staircases, and was therefore peculiarly suitable for purposes of retirement. It was decorated, with the picturesque daintiness of the French Court, in panels painted in imitation of Watteau, festooned with silk, embroidered with flowers. One or two cabinets supporting plate, and chairs richly embroidered in vari-coloured silk, completed the furniture. The supper was served on a small round table, with a costly service of china and Venetian glass.

Tina had accepted the invitation with pleasure. She had feared that this evening, when the work of another was being performed at the Imperial Theatre, to the exclusion of his great masterpiece, would have been a time of great depression with the Maestro, and she resolved to endeavour to cheer him. She had dressed herself with the greatest care, and without thought of cost. She had never looked so charming — every day seemed to mature her beauty. The supper was all that could have been expected or wished; nevertheless the Maestro was distrait and even sulky. Tina lavished her bewitching wiles and enchantments upon him in vain.

After the first course or two, which, it must be admitted, were served by the attendants in a somewhat perfunctory manner, the Maestro dismissed the servants, saying that the Signorina and he would prefer waiting upon themselves : dumb

waiters, containing wines and other acces-
sories, were placed by the table's side, and
the servants left the room.

Still the Maestro seemed ill at ease.
Tina, finding that her sallies were received
with a morose indifference, relapsed into
silence, and sat furtively glancing at her
companion, with a pouting, disconsolate
air which, it might have been thought,
would have been found irresistible even
by an ascetic.

At last the Maestro, after several futile
attempts, and with an awkward and embarrassed air, began :

"I have been thinking, Signora," he
said, "over my future plans, and I have
resolved not to try to get my music performed, at present at any rate, in any great
city. I am old and want rest. I propose

to travel for a few months. It will therefore not be necessary to take you from
Vienna."

His manner was so constrained, and his
resolution so unexpected, that the girl
looked at him with perplexity. It was, of
course, impossible for her, in her ignorance,
to perceive that what was troubling the
Maestro was the difficulty of concealing
from himself that he had accepted a bribe
to desert his art and his friend.

"Maestro," she said at last, "what can
you mean?—you to whom it has been
given to achieve such a success? How can
you talk of rest? What rest can be more
perfect than to listen to your own wonderful music? To see, to feel, the power of
your glorious art over others, over yourself?"

The Maestro hesitated and floundered worse than before. He was, as he had said himself, when under the influence of as noble feeling as he was capable of, a bad artist; but he had sufficient of the true instinct to be conscious of his bad work. He was ashamed of himself and of his *fainéantise.* He made a bungling business of it all round.

He had, before the Prince had made his offer, began to regret that in a moment of irritation he had been so precipitate in insisting upon leaving Vienna; but now that an offer of freedom, of a sojourn in Paris, of independent means, was made him, the proposal was too attractive to be declined. He felt, beside, that there was so much truth in the Prince's bitter phrase —when he was independent of his music, he felt certain that his music would be a great success.

" It will be better so, Faustina," he said at last ; "you will be happier here. You will have plenty to sing, plenty to teach you. The Prince will be pleased."

She was still looking at him wonderingly, but a smile was slowly growing in her eyes. She judged him by a nature as generous and unselfish as his was paltry and mean.

"You are saying this," she said, "for my sake. You fear that I shall suffer hardship and want. You sacrifice yourself —more than yourself—for me."

This turn in the conversation completed the vexation of the Maestro. When you are doing a particularly mean thing, nothing is more aggravating than to have noble and generous motives imputed to you;

and to have a very pretty woman offer herself to you, unreservedly, when motives of paltry selfishness render the offer unacceptable, is enough to provoke any man.

The old man lost his temper completely.

"Faustina," he said, "you are a fool. I have told you already that I intend to travel, without thinking of work or of pay. You must stay here. I shall not want you. You have everything here you can wish. The Prince is your lover. You have a brilliant future before you. Don't let me have any more trouble about you."

Still the girl could not believe that her friend and teacher meant to cast her off. She was looking at him wonderingly and sadly.

"Maestro," she said, "you are not well. You are cross and tired ; we will not speak of this any more to-night. This worry has made you ill. To-morrow you will see quite differently. You can never leave your art—and Tina."

This feminine persistency, as it seemed to him—this leaving a discussion open which it was absolutely necessary should be closed that night—was too much for the Maestro.

"I leave Vienna," he said brutally, "the day after to-morrow. I suppose that you will not insist on following me unin-vited. If so, I shall know what to do."

This tone and look revealed to the girl, at last, that she was cast off and discarded by the only man for whom she really cared. She threw herself on her knees beside his chair, and caught his hand.

"Maestro," she said passionately, "you

P

will not be so cruel! You will not leave me! What can I do? How can I live, without you? I cannot sing without you. I am your child. You took me out of the gutter; you taught me all I know; you made me all I am. I will do anything you tell me. I will not trouble you. I will not speak even! I care for no one except for you. I know you better, I can care for you, can serve you better, than they all. You will not be so cruel! You will not send me away from you."

The more passionately she spoke, the more rapid and fervent her utterance, the more fretful and irritated did the old man become. He pushed her roughly from him.

"Tina," he said again, "you are a fool. Get up from your knees. I don't want any of this stage-acting here."

He rose himself, and began to wander about the room, muttering and grumbling.

As he pushed her rudely from him, the girl rose and, retreating some steps from the table, gazed at him with a dazed, wondering look, as of one before whose eyes some strange unaccountable thing was happening.

She was standing, in her brilliant beauty and in her delicate and fantastic dress, her hands clasped before her. The jewels on her fingers and on her breast paled before the solemn glow of her wonderful eyes, which were dry, only from the intensity of her thought.

" No," she said at last, as it would seem in answer to some unspoken question. " No. There is nothing strange in this

A woman's heart is easily won. I am not the first, by many, who has found that out, too late."

It might have seemed impossible to one easily stirred, easily wrought upon by a woman's beauty—it would surely have seemed impossible to such a one that any could gaze on a sight like this and harbour a selfish thought; but the old man was perfectly unmoved.

" It is always the way," he said peevishly, "always the way with women; now we shall have a scene—tears—entreaties. I shall be called all manner of hard names for giving sensible advice."

And he turned his back upon the girl, and stood sullenly, gazing apparently upon one of the painted panels of the wall.

For about a minute there was a terrible

pause, then the curtains that veiled the *salon* were drawn forcibly back, and the groom of the chambers, who was a Frenchman, announced suddenly—

" *Monseigneur le Prince.*"

VIII.

THE Prince came forward smiling. The Maestro made a gesture of inexpressible relief. He shuffled off toward the still opened curtain, and, turning as he reached it, he bowed to the ground before his patron and his pupil, and disappeared through the opening as the servant let the curtain drop. We shall not care, I think, to see him again.

Faustina looked still more scared and bewildered than before at this sudden change of actors and of parts. She would gladly have left the room but she was incapable of anything of the kind—besides, where should she go ? The scene seemed to swim before her eyes, and the lights to flicker. She sank down on her chair again.

The Prince had never looked so well. He was flushed with excitement, and the habitual *insouciance* of his manner had given place to a reality and earnestness of purpose which rendered eloquent his every gesture and look. He was exquisitely dressed in silk, embroidered with flowers. The priceless lace at his wrists and throat accommodated itself, with a delicate fulness, to the soft outline of his dress and figure. His expression was full of kindliness and protection, but of kindliness delicate and refined. The girl's eyes were fascinated in spite of herself.

"Have you quarrelled with the Maestro, Tina?" said the Prince. "He seemed in a marvellous hurry to be gone."

Faustina made two or three ineffectual attempts to speak before she could find her voice. She burst into tears.

"He is cruel! cruel!" she said. "He does not love me. He will not have me any longer. He throws me away."

"Poor child!" said the Prince, "you will not be deserted. I am your friend; we are all your friends. The Maestro even will come back to you. He is cross and angry. When he finds how lost he is without you and your lovely voice, he will come back to you; you and he will carry all before you again."

"Speak to him, Highness!" cried the girl passionately. "You are kind and good to all—kinder than any one to me. Speak to him! do not let him go without me! He cannot live without his music, and no one surely can know his music so well as I, whom he has taught!"

She looked so indescribably attractive in her tears and her distress that the Prince wondered at the sight. "Let her go, indeed!".

"Tina," he said very kindly, "I fear that can hardly be. The Maestro is only going for a time. There is, in fact, no need that he should go at all. It is his own wish, his own wish, Tina. He is too old to make his way among strangers, and will soon come back. But you we cannot spare. You are too much a favourite with us all. We are too much accustomed to you: every one would miss you—the Princess and all; you must stay with us."

"I cannot stay," said the girl, looking earnestly and beseechingly at the Prince. "I want to go with him."

The Prince hesitated for a moment. In an instantaneous flash of thought the two paths lay open before him, plain and clear to be seen. Carricchio's warning struck him again with renewed force. The more terrible presage of Mark's death cast itself, ghostlike, before his steps. He could plead no excuse of self-deception : he saw the beauty and the danger of the way which lay before him on either hand. He hesitated for a moment, then he deliberately chose the lower path.

"Tina," he said, "I cannot spare you ; you must not go. You are mine—I love you ; you belong to me ;" and he stepped forward, as if to take her in his arms.

The girl sprang to her feet. She drew herself up to her full height, and her splendid eyes, expanded to their full orbit, flashed upon the Prince with a look of astonishment and reproach. With the entire power of her trained voice, which, magnificent as it was, could still but imperfectly render the reality of remonstrance and pathetic regret, she uttered but one word—" Prince !"

The cadence of her voice, trembling in the passionate intensity of musical tone, the whole power of her woman's nature, exerted to its full in expostulation and reproach—the magnetic force of her intense consciousness—struck upon the conscience and cultured taste of the Prince with crushing effect. He lost the perfectly serene tone of pose and demeanour which distinguished him and became him so well. He aged perceptibly, incredible as it may seem, ten years. The fatal step which he had taken was revealed to him in a moment as in a flash of light, with all the stain and taint with which it had tarnished the fair dream of finished art which he had conceived it possible to perfect. He was utterly demoralised and crushed. Mark's death was nothing to this. That had been a terrible mistake, but his part in it had been indirect, and his motive, at least so he flattered himself, comparatively high; but this action, so entirely his own, revealed to him, in its vulgar commonplaceness, by the glorious perfection of the girl's action and tone, withered him with a sense of irreparable failure and disgrace. He made one or two ineffectual attempts to rally; it was impossible—there was nothing for him but to leave the room.

Faustina was unconscious of his going. She found herself left alone. The situation was still not without its difficulties. She was alone, unattended by servants, she knew not where to go, how to leave the *Hôtel*. She lay for some time in a sort of swoon; then she rose and wandered from the room.

The only means of exit with which she was acquainted was through the curtains into the *salon*. She parted them and went out, hardly knowing what she did.

The vast *salon* was but dimly lighted, and no servants were to be seen; the whole house seemed silent and deserted

—more especially these state apartments.
She passed slowly and with faltering steps
down the slippery floor of the *salon*, with
its dimly-lighted candelabra of massive
silver and its half-seen portraits, and, opening the great door at the opposite end,
found herself in an antechamber which
communicated with a grand staircase, both
ascending and descending. To descend
was evidently useless—she could not go
out into the streets of Vienna alone at
night and in her fanciful dress. She went
up the wide staircase in the hope of finding some female domestics who would help
her; as she reached the next flight the
sound of music, subdued and solemn, fell
upon her ear. She knew enough of German music to know that it was the tune of
a hymn.

The door of the room from which the sound seemed to come stood partly open. She went in.

Before an harpsichord, with her hand carelessly passing over the keys, and her head turned at the sound of footsteps, stood the Princess Isoline. The light of a branched candelabra fell full upon her stately figure, revealing the compassionate, lofty expression of her beautiful face. The girl crossed the room towards her and fell on her knees at her feet.

"Child," said the Princess, "what is it? Why are you here?"

"I cannot tell," said the girl; and now at last she found it possible to weep. "I do not know what has happened. The Maestro has forsaken me, and I have insulted the Prince."

Gradually, in a broken way, she told her story, kneeling by the Princess, who stood serenely, her fingers still wandering over the harpsichord keys, her left hand caressing the girl's hair and cheek.

"He was a wonderful child," said the Princess at last, more to herself than to Faustina, for as she spoke she played again the simple notes of the Lutheran hymn. "He was truly a wonderful child. A very Christ-child, it seems to me, in his simple life and sudden death; for, though what he did was little, yet the lives of all of us seem different for his life—changed since his death. As for me, since his life crossed my path I have seen more, it seems to me, of the mercy of God and of Christ's working in paths and among lives where I never thought to look for it before."

Q

Faustina did not reply, and the Princess played several bars of the hymn before she spoke again.

"Do you not see," she said at last, "the blessing it has been also to my brother the Prince?—for the desire that he felt, surely a noble one, to refine the life of art by the sacred touch of religion—the effort that he made, though it seemed a failure, and was made—it may be, I dare not judge him—blindly, and in a mistaken fashion; yet this effort has to-night proved his own salvation, through you."

She stopped, and again the notes of the hymn sounded through the room.

"Carricchio was right," she went on, "when he told the Prince that you alone of all of us had solved the riddle, for on you alone has art exercised its supreme,

its magic touch, in drawing out and de-
veloping the emotions, the powers of the
soul. You alone possessed the perfect
gift of nature—the untainted well-spring
of natural life—which assimilated Mark's
spirit with your spirit, and reproduced his
life within your own."

Faustina dropped the Princess's hand,
which she had taken, and bent her head
still lower, as if shrinking from her kindly
praise.

" The Prince also had something of
this gift, and, in so far as he had, he built
up by his own action what, in his supreme
need, saved him from his lower self. I
have come to see that the world's virtues,
which, in my self-righteous isolation, I
despised, are often, as I blindly said to the
boy, nearer Christ's than my vaunted ones ;

that the world-spirit is often the Christ-spirit, and that, when we begin to see that His footsteps may be traced in paths where we little expect to find them, we shall no longer dare to talk of the secular life. Your little brother that died was not without his work, and the canary even was the type of a nobler life, even as Mark's death was the type of a nobler death.　In strange and unlooked-for ways the mission of sacrifice and love fulfils itself, and, living in the full light of its influence, we can never realise the blessing we have derived, the changed aspect of the race we have inherited, from the Cross of Christ."

IX.

THE next evening there was given, at the Imperial Palace, a ball and supper, to which none but *la haute noblesse* were invited. The dancing began with a brilliant Polonaise, which, headed by the Empress-Queen and her husband, passed through the rooms in stately procession, in singular and picturesque contrast and harmony with another faded and more solemn procession and array of figures in antique armour and dainty ruffs and doublets, and gold chains and princely mantles, the ancestral portraits who watched the formal slow dance-movement from the walls.

After the Polonaise came the supper, which was somewhat prolonged. The supper over, a minuet was danced, and afterward, the company being now happy and cheerful, and being, moreover, of sufficiently high and similar rank to dispense with somewhat of the rigid court etiquette, began to wander through the rooms in an informal manner, and to arrange *contre-danses* among themselves.

In those days the *contre-danse* had not hardened itself into the quadrille. It was danced, not in fours, but in sets of varying numbers, and of characters and figures mostly undefined.

In one of the great halls, recently erected by the Emperor-architect, Charles VI.,

in a different taste from the older rooms,
with marble floors and ceiling, and lined
with mirrors, a very large set, composed
of guests of the highest rank, was being
watched by no inconsiderable number of
their companions.

It is difficult to conceive a more magnificent or fascinating sight, reflected and
multiplied as it was by the mirrors on the
walls.

The Princess von Isenberg-Wertheim
was dancing with a young noble, a prince
of the House of Colleredo, a very handsome,
but gay and reckless, young man. The
dance was drawing to a close, the musicians,
playing one of the last figures, *La Pastorelle*,
to a very delicate and fine movement, to
which the dancers were devoting their
utmost, closest attention and skill.

As the Princess was standing by her partner, awaiting their turn to go down the dance, a slight movement caused her to turn her head, and she found the Count, her friend, standing close to her.

"I am sorry to interrupt, Princess," he said, in a low voice, "but I fear something serious has happened to the Prince. He cannot be found."

The Princess turned very pale. She caught her breath for a moment, then she said, in the same tone, "Where is Karl, the *Jager*?"

"I do not know," replied the Count. "I never thought of him."

"Then he is not here," said the Princess, with a relieved air. "If Karl is with him the Prince is safe."

The Count made a very slight move-

ment of his shoulders, but the Princess
turned serenely to the young man.

"We will finish the figure, Monseigneur," she said graciously; "then,
perhaps, you will excuse me."

"Nothing has happened to the Prince,
believe me," said the young man kindly,
as they moved down the room. "He has
doubtless gone on some private expedition
with his servant. He probably forgot to
leave a message, and will return to-morrow."

The Princess was so reassured, apparently, by these reflections that she remained
for the final figure of the dance. Then
she left the palace, and, declining the
Count's company, drove to her *Hôtel* alone.

She was more strangely moved than
she could have explained to herself. She
was, indeed, frightened and perplexed by

her own feelings. She felt herself influenced by an hitherto unrecognised power, and, as it were, driven onwards by an overpowering impulse, not her own.

Returning, as she did, at an unexpected hour, her women were not in waiting for her, and, leaving the servants who had accompanied her from the palace in the hall of the *Hôtel*, she wandered up the great staircase alone. The corridors and rooms were dimly lighted, and a perfect stillness reigned through the house.

The Princess ascended slowly towards her own apartment, where she expected to find some, at least, of her dressers, and in so doing, in a dimly-lighted corridor, she passed the rooms allotted to her children. The thought of them was not, indeed, in her mind when, as she passed a door, she fancied that she heard a suppressed, continued crying, as of children in distress. Still more moved and troubled by this faint pathetic sound she opened the door and went in. The room was an antechamber, and both it and the apartment beyond were dark. The Princess procured a small lamp from the corridor and entered the suite of rooms.

In the bedchamber beyond the antechamber she found the children, both sitting up in one bed, clasped in each other's arms, and crying quietly. The little boy had evidently come for shelter and comfort to his sister's bed.

"What is the matter, children?" said the Princess, in a tone which seemed to the little ones strangely soft and kind. "Why are you not asleep?"

The children had ceased crying, and were looking at her wonderingly as she stood in her jewels and ball-dress, a brilliant scarf of Indian work hanging from her arm, the lamp in her hand. They hardly knew whether it was their mother, whom they saw so seldom, or some serene ethereal visitant, who resembled her in face and form.

The little Princess, however, with the self-possession of her class, apparently left this point undecided, and began in her quiet, stately little way to explain.

"It was dark," she said, "and we were asleep, Fritz and I, and we both dreamed the same dream. We thought that we were walking in a beautiful garden, where there were trees, and flowers, and butter-flies, and wide cascades of water, in which

rainbows were shining ; and while we were
playing there, and were very happy chasing
the butterflies, the Herr Tutor, who was an
angel, and who went to heaven, came and
took us by the hand ; and, when we saw
his face, we knew that he is an angel now;
and he led us through the garden, and
talked to us of many things—of God, and
of angels, and of heaven—just as he used
to do.   But I saw that, though he talked so
pleasantly, he was leading us out of this
pleasant garden, and the flowers grew dim,
and the butterflies flew away, and the sky
became very dark.   And he led us quite
out of the garden into a burial-ground,
where there were tombs, and open graves,
and crosses, and tall dark trees that bore
no flower ; and the Herr Tutor told us not
to be afraid, and led us on through the

graves without speaking any more. He led us into the midst of the burial-ground, and in the midst of the burial-ground there was a Calvary, and at the foot of the Calvary there was a bier. And on the bier we saw you and papa lying quite straight and still, and we thought that you were dead. And the Herr Tutor vanished away; and we were so frightened that we cried. And we knelt side by side, and prayed to the Christ that He would come down. And the Christ came down from the cross, and came to the bier, and touched it, and you and papa stood up beautiful and smiling, and came towards us with outstretched hands, and the Christ vanished away. And we were so glad that we awoke ; and it was dark, and there was no Christ, and no Herr Tutor, who is an angel, and no papa, and no one to tell us what to do or where to go."

As the little Princess ceased some servants came in, with whispered explanations and apologies. The Princess went to her own room. She had not known what to say to the child; indeed, she hardly knew what had passed. She allowed herself to be undressed, and lay down.

But, in the deep silence of the hours that preceded the dawn, an overpowering restlessness took possession of her. A sense of strange forces and influences, to which she was utterly unaccustomed, seemed present to her spirit: a crowd of fair and heavenly existences, which seemed to follow on the steps of that singular boy who had first attracted her wearied fancy, the Signorina's singing, which had stamped this impression upon her mind, the strange tenderness she had been conscious of, the renewed sense of her husband's grace and beauty, his alarming absence, her children's mystical dream. A new world seemed to open to her. She felt how poor and bare her life had been, how deserted by these gracious creatures of the imagination, how unblessed by the purest, the truest art—the art of pathos and of love.

With the streaks of dawn that stole into the chamber she was conscious of an irrepressible desire that took possession of her to rise and go forth. An irresistible power seemed to draw her to follow : she rose, and, dressing herself in such clothes as were at hand, she went out.

The house itself was quite still, but faintly in the distance might be heard the sound of a bell. In so religious a Court as that of Vienna there were private chapels attached to most of the houses of the nobility, and there was one attached to a neighbouring palace, to which there was a private communication with the *Hôtel* taken by the Prince.

Following the sound of the bell the Princess traversed several passages, and reached at last a staircase, down which she turned. As she reached the first landing two women came out from an open door. They started at the sight of the Princess. They were the Princess Isoline and Faustina.

"Is it you, Princess?" said the former. "What has called you up so early?"

"Are you going to the chapel, Isoline?'
said the Princess.   "May I come with
you ?"

The three ladies entered the chapel by
a private door, which led them to a pew
behind the stalls.   Upon the original
Gothic stone - work and tracery of the
chapel, which was very old, had been
introduced rococo work in mahogany and
brass, angels and trumpets and scrolls.
The stalls and organs were covered with
filigree work of this description, the windows filled with paintings in the same
florid and incongruous taste.   There were
few persons in the chapel, most of them
being ladies from the adjoining palaces,
together with a few musicians, for the
musical part of the service was care-

fully performed by a large and well-paid staff.

Two of the ladies were Protestant, the third, Faustina, a Catholic of a very un-developed type; but the music of the Mass spoke a mysterious language, recognisable to hearts of every creed.

Before the altar, laden with gilded plate and lighted with candles in silver sconces, the priest said Mass. Above him, in the window, painted in a lovely Italian land-scape full of figures, with towns and castles and mountain ranges and market-people with horses and cattle, were represented, in careful and minute painting, the three Marys before the empty tomb.

"The City of the Sunlight," sang the choir, in an elaborate anthem, with an allegro movement of the tenors that spoke of sunshine amid the grass and flowers and flashing sea, of the breezy south wind upon rippling water and golden hair; and after them the bass recitative, with a positive assurance that knew no doubt, asserted "The gates—the gates of it are many—many," which the tenors and altos, with a sudden inspiration, interpreted, " God's purposes fulfilled—fulfilled in many ways;" and the whole choir, in a minor key, as with hushed and awe-struck voices, completed the theme, " But the end is union in the heart—the heart of the Crucifix; in the City—the City of the Saints. "

*　　*　　*　　*　　*

On her return from the chapel a note from the Prince was put into the Princess's hand. It merely stated that he was gone to Hernhuth to the Count Zinzendorf. It had been written at a tavern in the environs of the city, after his sudden determination had been formed the day before, and had been entrusted to a servant of the inn to deliver. He had arrived at the *Hôtel* after the Princess had left, and, on asking for her Highness, had been told by a careless porter that she was at the Palace. Wandering about the Palace courts late at night he had been arrested as a suspicious person, and kept prisoner till the morning.

In course of time (posts were slow in those days) the Princess received a long letter from her husband, giving an account of Hernhuth, and of his conversations with the Count, and concluding with these words :—

" From all this you will, doubtless, conclude that Hernhuth does not suit me very well, and that the Count and I do not always agree.   It would be more after Isoline's taste.   I like the children's dream, as you tell it, best.   We have been dead, and laid upon a bier; but we will, please God, live hereafter for the children and the Christ."

THE END.

Printed by R. & R. CLARK, *Edinburgh.*

ENGLISH MEN OF LETTERS.

Edited by JOHN MORLEY.

Crown 8vo.   Cloth, 1s. 6d. ; sewed, 1s.

ADDISON.
By W. J. COURTHOPE.

BACON.
By Dean CHURCH.

BENTLEY.
By Professor R. C. JEBB.

BUNYAN.
By J. A. FROUDE.

BURKE.
By JOHN MORLEY.

BURNS.
By Principal SHAIRP.

BYRON.
By Professor NICHOL.

CHAUCER.
By Professor A. W. WARD.

COLERIDGE.
By H. D. TRAILL.

COWPER.
By GOLDWIN SMITH.

DEFOE.
By W. MINTO.

DE QUINCEY.
By Professor MASSON.

DICKENS.
By Professor A. W. WARD.

DRYDEN.
By G. SAINTSBURY.

FIELDING.
By AUSTIN DOBSON.

GIBBON.
By J. C. MORISON.

GOLDSMITH.
By WILLIAM BLACK.

GRAY.
By EDMUND GOSSE.

HAWTHORNE.
By HENRY JAMES.

HUME.
By Professor HUXLEY, F.R.S.

JOHNSON.
By LESLIE STEPHEN.

KEATS.
By SIDNEY COLVIN.

LAMB, CHARLES.
By Rev. A. AINGER.

LANDOR.
By SIDNEY COLVIN.

LOCKE.
By THOMAS FOWLER.

MACAULAY.
By J. C. MORISON.

MILTON.
By MARK PATTISON.

POPE.
By LESLIE STEPHEN.

SCOTT.
By R. H. HUTTON.

SHELLEY.
By J. A. SYMONDS.

SHERIDAN.
By Mrs. OLIPHANT.

SIDNEY.
By JOHN A. SYMONDS.

SOUTHEY.
By Professor DOWDEN.

SPENSER.
By Dean CHURCH.

STERNE.
By H. D. TRAILL.

SWIFT.
By LESLIE STEPHEN.

THACKERAY.
By ANTHONY TROLLOPE.

WORDSWORTH.
By F. W. H. MYERS.

CARLYLE. By JOHN NICHOL. Crown 8vo.   2s. 6d.

MACMILLAN AND CO., LONDON.

Golden Treasury Series.

Uniformly printed with Vignette Titles by Sir J. E. MILLAIS, Sir NOEL PATON,
T. WOOLNER, W. HOLMAN HUNT, ARTHUR HUGHES, etc.,
engraved on Steel.

In uniform binding, Pott 8vo, 2s. 6d. each, net.

THE GOLDEN TREASURY OF THE BEST SONGS AND
LYRICAL POEMS IN THE ENGLISH LANGUAGE. Selected and arranged,
with Notes, by Professor F. T. PALGRAVE. *Large Paper Edition.* 8vo. 10s. 6d. net.

THE CHILDREN'S TREASURY OF LYRICAL POETRY.
Selected by Professor F. T. PALGRAVE.

THE CHILDREN'S GARLAND FROM THE BEST POETS.
Selected by COVENTRY PATMORE.

POEMS OF WORDSWORTH. Chosen and edited by MATTHEW
ARNOLD. *Large Paper Edition.* 8vo. 9s.

POETRY OF BYRON. Chosen and arranged by MATTHEW ARNOLD.
Large Paper Edition. 9s.

POEMS OF SHELLEY. Edited by S. A. BROOKE. *Large Paper
Edition.* 8vo. 12s. 6d.

THE POETICAL WORKS OF JOHN KEATS. Edited by
Professor F. T. PALGRAVE.

CHRYSOMELA. A Selection from the Lyrical Poems of Robert
Herrick. By Professor F. T. PALGRAVE.

SELECTED POEMS OF MATTHEW ARNOLD.

BALLADS, LYRICS, AND SONNETS. From the Works of
HENRY W. LONGFELLOW.

MACMILLAN AND CO., LONDON.

Golden Treasury Series—*Continued.*

LYRIC LOVE : An Anthology. Edited by WILLIAM WATSON.

SCOTTISH SONG. Compiled by MARY CARLYLE AITKEN.

THE SONG BOOK. Words and Tunes selected and arranged by JOHN HULLAH.

THE BALLAD BOOK. Edited by WILLIAM ALLINGHAM.

THE FAIRY BOOK. Selected by Mrs. CRAIK.

THE JEST BOOK. Arranged by MARK LEMON.

SHAKESPEARE'S SONGS AND SONNETS. Edited, with Notes, by Professor F. T. PALGRAVE.

LAMB'S TALES FROM SHAKESPEARE. Edited by Rev. ALFRED AINGER, M.A.

SELECTIONS FROM COWPER'S POEMS. With an Introduction by Mrs. OLIPHANT.

LETTERS OF WILLIAM COWPER. Edited, with Introduction, by Rev. W. BENHAM.

THE BOOK OF PRAISE. Selected by ROUNDELL, EARL OF SELBORNE.

THE SUNDAY BOOK OF POETRY FOR THE YOUNG. Selected by C. F. ALEXANDER.

MACMILLAN AND CO., LONDON.

𝕲𝖔𝖑𝖉𝖊𝖓 𝕿𝖗𝖊𝖆𝖘𝖚𝖗𝖞 𝕾𝖊𝖗𝖎𝖊𝖘—*Continued.*

LA LYRE FRANÇAISE. Selected and arranged, with Notes, by G. MASSON.

DEUTSCHE LYRIK. The Golden Treasury of the Best German Lyrical Poems. Selected by Dr. BUCHHEIM.

BALLADEN UND ROMANZEN. Being a Selection of the best German Ballads and Romances. Edited, with Introduction and Notes, by Dr. BUCHHEIM.

THEOCRITUS, BION, AND MOSCHUS. Rendered into English Prose by ANDREW LANG. *Large Paper Edition.* 9s.

THE REPUBLIC OF PLATO. Translated by LL. DAVIES, M.A., and D. J. VAUGHAN. *Large Paper Edition.* 8vo. 10s. 6d. net.

THE TRIAL AND DEATH OF SOCRATES. Being the Euthyphron, Apology, Crito, and Phædo of Plato. Translated by F. J. CHURCH.

PLATO—PHAEDRUS, LYSIS, AND PROTAGORAS. A New Translation, by J. WRIGHT.

BACON'S ESSAYS, AND COLOURS OF GOOD AND EVIL. With Notes and Glossarial Index by W. ALDIS WRIGHT, M.A. *Large Paper Edition.* 8vo. 10s. 6d. net.

THE CAVALIER AND HIS LADY. Selections from the Works of the First Duke and Duchess of Newcastle. With an Introductory Essay by EDWARD JENKINS.

THE PILGRIM'S PROGRESS FROM THIS WORLD TO THAT WHICH IS TO COME. By JOHN BUNYAN. *Large Paper Edition.* 8vo. 10s. 6d. net.

SIR THOMAS BROWNE'S RELIGIO MEDICI; LETTERS TO A FRIEND, ETC., AND CHRISTIAN MORALS. Edited by W. A. GREENHILL, M.D.

MACMILLAN AND CO., LONDON.

Golden Treasury Series—*Continued.*

THE ESSAYS OF JOSEPH ADDISON. Chosen and edited by JOHN RICHARD GREEN.

SELECTIONS FROM WALTER SAVAGE LANDOR. Edited by SIDNEY COLVIN.

TOM BROWN'S SCHOOL DAYS. By an OLD BOY.

BALTHASAR GRACIAN'S ART OF WORLDLY WISDOM. Translated by J. JACOBS.

THE SPEECHES AND TABLE-TALK OF THE PROPHET MOHAMMAD. Translated by STANLEY LANE-POOLE.

THE STORY OF THE CHRISTIANS AND MOORS IN SPAIN. By CHARLOTTE M. YONGE.

A BOOK OF GOLDEN DEEDS OF ALL TIMES AND ALL COUNTRIES. By C. M. YONGE.

A BOOK OF WORTHIES. By C. M. YONGE.

A BOOK OF GOLDEN THOUGHTS. By Sir HENRY ATTWELL.

GOLDEN TREASURY PSALTER. THE STUDENT'S EDITION. Being an Edition with Briefer Notes of "The Psalms Chronologically Arranged by Four Friends."

THEOLOGIA GERMANICA. Translated by S. WINKWORTH. Preface by C. KINGSLEY.

MACMILLAN AND CO., LONDON.

MACMILLAN'S THREE-AND-SIXPENNY LIBRARY OF BOOKS BY POPULAR AUTHORS

Crown 8vo.

*T*HIS SERIES comprises over four hundred volumes in various departments of Literature. Prominent among them is an attractive edition of **The Works of Thackeray,** *issued under the editorship of Mr. Lewis Melville. It contains all the Original Illustrations, and includes a great number of scattered pieces and illustrations which have not hitherto appeared in any collected edition of the works.* **The Works of Charles Dickens,** *reprinted from the first editions, with all the Original Illustrations, and with Introductions, Biographical and Bibliographical, by Charles Dickens the Younger, and an attractive edition of* **The Novels of Charles Lever,** *illustrated by Phiz and G. Cruik-*

shank, have also a place in the Library. The attention of book buyers may be especially directed to **The Border Edition of the Waverley Novels,** *edited by Mr. Andrew Lang, which, with its large type and convenient form, and its copious illustrations by well-known artists, possesses features which place it in the forefront of editions now obtainable of the famous novels.* **The Works of Mr. Thomas Hardy,** *including the poems, have also been added to the Three-and-Sixpenny Library.*

Among other works by notable contemporary authors will be found those of Mr. F. Marion Crawford, Rolf Boldrewood, Mr. H. G. Wells, Mrs. Gertrude Atherton, Mr. Egerton Castle, Mr. A. E. W. Mason, Maarten Maartens, *and* Miss Rosa Nouchette Carey; *while among the productions of an earlier period may be mentioned the works of* Charles Kingsley, Frederick Denison Maurice, Thomas Hughes, *and* Dean Farrar; *and the novels and tales of* Charlotte M. Yonge, Mrs. Craik, *and* Mrs. Oliphant.

THE

WORKS OF THACKERAY

Reprints of the First Editions, with all the Original Illustrations, and with Facsimiles of Wrappers, etc.

Messrs. MACMILLAN & CO., Limited, beg leave to invite the attention of book buyers to the Edition of THE WORKS OF THACKERAY in their Three-and-Sixpenny Library, which is the Completest Edition of the Author's Works that has been placed on the market.

The Publishers have been fortunate in securing the services of Mr. LEWIS MELVILLE, the well-known Thackeray Expert. With his assistance they have been able to include in this Edition a great number of scattered pieces from Thackeray's pen, and illus- trations from his pencil which have not hitherto been contained in any collected edition of the works. Mr. Melville has read all the sheets as they passed through the press, and collated them carefully with the original editions. He has also provided Biblio- graphical Introductions and occasional Footnotes.

List of the Series.

VOL.

1. Vanity Fair. With 190 Illustrations.

2. The History of Pendennis. With 180 Illustrations.

3. The Newcomes. With 167 Illustrations.

4. The History of Henry Esmond.

5. The Virginians. With 148 Illustrations.

6. Barry Lyndon and Catherine. With 4 Illustrations.

7. The Paris and Irish Sketch Books. With 63 Illustrations.

THACKERAY'S WORKS—*continued.*

VOL.

8. Christmas Books—Mrs. Perkins's
Ball: Our Street: Dr. Birch and his Young
Friends: The Kickleburys on the Rhine: The
Rose and the Ring. With 127 Illustrations.

9. Burlesques: From Cornhill to Grand
Cairo: and Juvenilia. With 84 Illustrations.

10. The Book of Snobs, and other Contributions to *Punch*. With 159 Illustrations.

11. The Yellowplush Correspondence:
Jeames's Diary: The Great Hoggarty Diamond: Etc.
With 47 Illustrations.

12. Critical Papers in Literature.

13. Critical Papers in Art; Stubbs's Calen-
dar: Barber Cox. With 99 Illustrations.

14. Lovel the Widower, and other Stories.
With 40 Illustrations.

15. The Fitz-Boodle Papers (including
Men's Wives), and various Articles. 8 Illustrations.

16. The English Humourists of the 18th
Century: The Four Georges: Etc. 45 Illustrations.

17. Travels in London: Letters to a Young
Man about Town: and other Contributions to *Punch*
(1845—1850). With 73 Illustrations.

18. Ballads and Verses, and Miscellaneous
Contributions to *Punch*. With 78 Illustrations.

19. A Shabby Genteel Story, and The
Adventures of Philip. With Illustrations.

20. Roundabout Papers and Denis Duval.
With Illustrations.

MACMILLAN'S

EDITION OF THACKERAY

SOME OPINIONS OF THE PRESS

EXPOSITORY TIMES.—"An edition to do credit even to this publishing house, and not likely to be surpassed until they surpass it with a cheaper and better themselves."

WHITEHALL REVIEW.—"Never before has such a cheap and excellent edition of Thackeray been seen."

ACADEMY.—"A better one-volume edition at three shillings and sixpence could not be desired."

GRAPHIC.—"In its plain but pretty blue binding is both serviceable and attractive."

DAILY GRAPHIC.—"An excellent, cheap reprint."

PALL MALL GAZETTE.—"The size of the books is handy, paper and printing are good, and the binding, which is of blue cloth, is simple but tasteful. Altogether the publishers are to be congratulated upon a reprint which ought to be popular."

GLOBE.—"The paper is thin but good, the type used is clear to read, and the binding is neat and effective."

LADY'S PICTORIAL.—"The paper is good, the type clear and large, and the binding tasteful. Messrs. Macmillan are to be thanked for so admirable and inexpensive an edition of our great satirist."

WORLD.—"Nothing could be better than the new edition."

BLACK AND WHITE.—"The more one sees of the edition the more enamoured of it he becomes. It is so good and neat, immaculate as to print, and admirably bound."

SCOTSMAN.—"This admirable edition."

LITERARY WORLD.—"The paper and printing and general get up are everything that one could desire."

ST. JAMES'S GAZETTE.—"A clear and pretty edition."

THE

WORKS OF DICKENS

Reprints of the First Editions, with all the original Illustrations, and with Introductions, Biographical and Bibliographical, by CHARLES DICKENS the Younger.

1. THE PICKWICK PAPERS.   With 50 Illustrations.
2. OLIVER TWIST.   With 27 Illustrations.
3. NICHOLAS NICKLEBY.   With 44 Illustrations.
4. MARTIN CHUZZLEWIT.   With 41 Illustrations.
5. THE OLD CURIOSITY SHOP.   With 97 Illustrations.
6. BARNABY RUDGE.   With 76 Illustrations.
7. DOMBEY AND SON.   With 40 Illustrations.
8. CHRISTMAS BOOKS.   With 65 Illustrations.
9. SKETCHES BY BOZ.   With 44 Illustrations.
10. DAVID COPPERFIELD.   With 40 Illustrations.
11. AMERICAN NOTES AND PICTURES FROM ITALY.   With 4 Illustrations.
12. THE LETTERS OF CHARLES DICKENS.
13. BLEAK HOUSE.   With 43 Illustrations.
14. LITTLE DORRIT.   With 40 Illustrations.
15. A TALE OF TWO CITIES.   With 15 Illustrations.
16. GREAT EXPECTATIONS;   AND HARD TIMES.
17. OUR MUTUAL FRIEND.   With 40 Illustrations.

MACMILLAN'S

EDITION OF DICKENS

SOME OPINIONS OF THE PRESS

ATHENÆUM.—" Handy in form, well printed, illustrated with reduced re-productions of the original plates, introduced with bibliographical notes by the novelist's son, and above all issued at a most moderate price, this edition will appeal successfully to a large number of readers."

SPEAKER.—" We do not think there exists a better edition."

MORNING POST.—" The edition will be highly appreciated."

SCOTSMAN.—" This reprint offers peculiar attractions. Of a handy size, in one volume, of clear, good-sized print, and with its capital comic illustrations, it is a volume to be desired."

NEWCASTLE CHRONICLE.—" The most satisfactory edition of the book that has been issued."

GLASGOW HERALD.—" None of the recent editions of Dickens can be compared with that which Messrs. Macmillan inaugurate with the issue of *Pickwick.* . . . Printed in a large, clear type, very readable."

GLOBE.—" They have used an admirably clear type and good paper, and the binding is unexceptionable. . . . May be selected as the most desirable cheap edition of the immortal ' Papers ' that has ever been offered to the public."

MANCHESTER EXAMINER.—" These volumes have a unique interest, for with each there is the story of its origin."

QUEEN.—" A specially pleasant and convenient form in which to re-read Dickens."

STAR.—" This new ' Dickens Series,' with its reproductions of the original illustrations, is a joy to the possessor."

Complete in Twenty-four Volumes.   Crown 8vo, tastefully bound in green cloth, gilt.   Price 3s. 6d. each.

In special cloth binding, flat backs, gilt tops.   Supplied in Sets only of 24 volumes.   Price £4 4s.

Also an edition with all the 250 original etchings.   In 24 volumes. Crown 8vo, gilt tops.   Price 6s. each.

THE LARGE TYPE
BORDER EDITION OF THE
WAVERLEY NOVELS

EDITED WITH

INTRODUCTORY ESSAYS AND NOTES

BY

ANDREW LANG
SUPPLEMENTING THOSE OF THE AUTHOR.

With Two Hundred and Fifty New and Original Illustrations by Eminent Artists.

BY the kind permission of the Hon. Mrs. MAXWELL-SCOTT, of Abbotsford, the great-granddaughter of Sir WALTER, the MSS. and other material at Abbotsford were examined by Mr. ANDREW LANG during the preparation of his Introductory Essays and Notes to the Series, so that the BORDER EDITION may be said to contain all the results of the latest researches as to the composition of the Waverley Novels.

The Border Waverley

The Border Waverley

12. KENILWORTH.   With 12 Illustrations by AD. LALAUZE.

13. THE PIRATE.   With 10 Illustrations by W. E. LOCKHART, R.S.A., SAM BOUGH, R.S.A., HERBERT DICKSEE, W. STRANG, LOCKHART BOGLE, C. J. HOLMES, and F. S. WALKER.

14. THE FORTUNES OF NIGEL.   With 10 Illustrations by JOHN PETTIE, R.A., and R. W. MACBETH, A.R.A.

15. PEVERIL OF THE PEAK.   With 15 Illustrations by W. Q. ORCHARDSON, R.A. JOHN PETTIE, R.A., F. DADD, R.I., ARTHUR HOPKINS, A.R.W.S., and S. L. WOOD.

16. QUENTIN DURWARD.   With 12 Illustrations by AD. LALAUZE.

17. ST. RONAN'S WELL.   With 10 Illustrations by Sir G. REID, P.R.S.A., R. W. MACBETH, A.R.A., W. HOLE, R.S.A., and A. FORESTIER.

18. REDGAUNTLET.   With 12 Illustrations by Sir JAMES D. LINTON, P.R.I., JAMES ORROCK, R.I., SAM BOUGH, R.S.A., W. HOLE, R.S.A., G. HAY, R.S.A., T. SCOTT, A.R.S.A., W. BOUCHER, and FRANK SHORT.

19. THE BETROTHED and THE TALISMAN.   With 10 Illustrations by HERBERT DICKSEE, WAL. PAGET, and J. LE BLANT.

20. WOODSTOCK.   With 10 Illustrations by W. HOLE. R.S.A.

21. THE FAIR MAID OF PERTH.   With 10 Illustrations by Sir G. REID, P.R.S.A., JOHN PETTIE, R.A., R. W. MACBETH, A.R.A., and ROBERT HERDMAN, R.S.A.

22. ANNE OF GEIERSTEIN.   With 10 Illustrations by R. DE LOS RIOS.

23. COUNT ROBERT OF PARIS and THE SURGEON'S DAUGHTER.   With 10 Illustrations by W. HATHERELL, R.I., and W. B. WOLLEN, R.I.

24. CASTLE DANGEROUS, CHRONICLES OF THE CANON-GATE, ETC.   With 10 Illustrations by H. MACBETH-RAE-BURN and G. D. ARMOUR

The Border Waverley
SOME OPINIONS OF THE PRESS

TIMES.—"It would be difficult to find in these days a more com·petent and sympathetic editor of Scott than his countryman, the brilliant and versatile man of letters who has undertaken the task, and if any proof were wanted either of his qualifications or of his skill and discretion in displaying them, Mr. Lang has furnished it abundantly in his charming Introduction to 'Waverley.' The editor's own notes are judiciously sparing, but conspicuously to the point, and they are very discreetly separated from those of the author, Mr. Lang's laudable purpose being to illustrate and explain Scott, not to make the notes a pretext for displaying his own critical faculty and literary erudition. The illustrations by various competent hands are beautiful in themselves and beautifully executed, and, altogether, the 'Border Edition' of the Waverley Novels bids fair to become the classical edition of the great Scottish classic."

SPECTATOR.—"We trust that this fine edition of our greatest and most poetical of novelists will attain, if it has not already done so, the high popularity it deserves. To all Scott's lovers it is a pleasure to know that, despite the daily and weekly inrush of ephemeral fiction, the sale of his works is said by the booksellers to rank next below Tennyson's in poetry, and above that of everybody else in prose."

ATHENÆUM.—"The handsome 'Border Edition' has been brought to a successful conclusion. The publisher deserves to be complimented on the manner in which the edition has been printed and illustrated, and Mr. Lang on the way in which he has performed his portion of the work. His introductions have been tasteful and readable ; he has not overdone his part ; and, while he has supplied much useful information, he has by no means overburdened the volumes with notes."

NOTES AND QUERIES.—"This spirited and ambitious enterprise has been conducted to a safe termination, and the most ideal edition of the Waverley Novels in existence is now completed."

SATURDAY REVIEW.—"Of all the many collections of the Waverley Novels, the 'Border Edition' is incomparably the most handsome and the most desirable. . . . Type, paper, illustrations, are altogether admirable."

MAGAZINE OF ART.—"Size, type, paper, and printing, to say nothing of the excessively liberal and charming introduction of the illustrations, make this perhaps the most desirable edition of Scott ever issued on this side of the Border."

DAILY CHRONICLE.—"There is absolutely no fault to be found with it, as to paper, type, or arrangement."

THE WORKS OF
THOMAS HARDY
Collected Edition

1. TESS OF THE D'URBERVILLES.
2. FAR FROM THE MADDING CROWD.
3. THE MAYOR OF CASTERBRIDGE.
4. A PAIR OF BLUE EYES.
5. TWO ON A TOWER.
6. THE RETURN OF THE NATIVE.
7. THE WOODLANDERS.
8. JUDE THE OBSCURE.
9. THE TRUMPET-MAJOR.
10. THE HAND OF ETHELBERTA.
11. A LAODICEAN.
12. DESPERATE REMEDIES.
13. WESSEX TALES.
14. LIFE'S LITTLE IRONIES.
15. A GROUP OF NOBLE DAMES.
16. UNDER THE GREENWOOD TREE.
17. THE WELL-BELOVED.
18. WESSEX POEMS, and other Verses.
19. POEMS OF THE PAST AND THE PRESENT.

THE WORKS OF

CHARLES KINGSLEY

WESTWARD HO !

HYPATIA ; or, New Foes with an old Face.

TWO YEARS AGO.

ALTON LOCKE, Tailor and Poet.   An Autobiography.

HEREWARD THE WAKE, "Last of the English."

YEAST : A Problem.

POEMS : including The Saint's Tragedy, Andromeda, Songs
Ballads, etc.

THE WATER-BABIES : A Fairy Tale for a Land-Baby.   With
Illustrations by LINLEY SAMBOURNE.

THE HEROES ; or, Greek Fairy Tales for my Children.   With
Illustrations by the Author.

GLAUCUS ; or, The Wonders of the Shore.   With Illustrations.

MADAM HOW AND LADY WHY ; or, First Lessons in
Earth Lore for Children.   With Illustrations.

AT LAST.   A Christmas in the West Indies.   With Illustrations.

THE HERMITS.

HISTORICAL LECTURES AND ESSAYS.

PLAYS AND PURITANS, and other Historical Essays.

THE ROMAN AND THE TEUTON.

PROSE IDYLLS, New and Old.

SCIENTIFIC LECTURES AND ESSAYS.

SANITARY AND SOCIAL LECTURES AND ESSAYS.

LITERARY AND GENERAL LECTURES AND ESSAYS.

ALL SAINTS' DAY : and other Sermons.

DISCIPLINE : and other Sermons.

THE GOOD NEWS OF GOD.   Sermons.

GOSPEL OF THE PENTATEUCH.

SERMONS FOR THE TIMES.

VILLAGE SERMONS, AND TOWN AND COUNTRY
SERMONS.

THE WATER OF LIFE : and other Sermons.

WESTMINSTER SERMONS.

THE NOVELS

OF

F. MARION CRAWFORD

THE NOVELS

OF

F. MARION CRAWFORD

THE NOVELS

OF

ROLF BOLDREWOOD

1. ROBBERY UNDER ARMS: A Story of Life and Adventure in the Bush and in the Gold-fields of Australia.

2. A MODERN BUCCANEER.

3. THE MINER'S RIGHT: A Tale of the Australian Gold-fields.

4. THE SQUATTER'S DREAM.

5. A SYDNEY-SIDE SAXON.

6. A COLONIAL REFORMER.

7. NEVERMORE.

8. PLAIN LIVING: A Bush Idyll.

9. MY RUN HOME.

10. THE SEALSKIN CLOAK.

11. THE CROOKED STICK ; or, Pollie's Probation.

12. OLD MELBOURNE MEMORIES.

13. A ROMANCE OF CANVAS TOWN, and other Stories.

14. WAR TO THE KNIFE ; or, Tangata Maori.

15. BABES IN THE BUSH.

16. IN BAD COMPANY, and other Stories.

By H. G. WELLS
THE PLATTNER STORY: and others.
TALES OF SPACE AND TIME.
THE STOLEN BACILLUS: and other Incidents.
THE INVISIBLE MAN. A Grotesque Romance.
LOVE AND MR. LEWISHAM. A Story of a very
Young Couple.
WHEN THE SLEEPER WAKES.
THE FIRST MEN IN THE MOON.
TWELVE STORIES AND A DREAM.
THE FOOD OF THE GODS AND HOW IT
Came to Earth.
KIPPS: The Story of a Simple Soul.

By A. E. W. MASON
THE COURTSHIP OF MORRICE BUCKLER.
THE PHILANDERERS.
MIRANDA OF THE BALCONY.

By EGERTON CASTLE
"LA BELLA": and others. | "YOUNG APRIL."
MARSHFIELD THE OBSERVER.

By AGNES and EGERTON CASTLE
THE BATH COMEDY.
THE PRIDE OF JENNICO. Being a Memoir of
Captain Basil Jennico.
THE SECRET ORCHARD.

By MAARTEN MAARTENS
THE GREATER GLORY. A Story of High Life.
MY LADY NOBODY. A Novel.
GOD'S FOOL. A Koopstad Story.
THE SIN OF JOOST AVELINGH. A Dutch Story.
HER MEMORY. | AN OLD MAID'S LOVE.

THE NOVELS OF

ROSA N. CAREY

Over 700,000 of these works have been printed.

THE NOVELS OF

ROSA N. CAREY

Over 700,000 of these works have been printed.

12. RUE WITH A DIFFERENCE. 24th Thousand.
13. THE HIGHWAY OF FATE. 23rd Thousand.
14. ONLY THE GOVERNESS. 37th Thousand.
15. LOVER OR FRIEND? 27th Thousand.
16. BASIL LYNDHURST. 24th Thousand.
17. SIR GODFREY'S GRAND-DAUGHTERS. 25th Thousand.
18. THE OLD, OLD STORY. 27th Thousand.
19. THE MISTRESS OF BRAE FARM. 30th Thousand.
20. MRS. ROMNEY and "BUT MEN MUST WORK." 14th Thousand.
21. OTHER PEOPLE'S LIVES. 5th Thousand.
22. HERB OF GRACE. 25th Thousand.
23. A PASSAGE PERILOUS. 22nd Thousand.
24. AT THE MOORINGS. 21st Thousand.
25. THE HOUSEHOLD OF PETER. 21st Thousand.
26. NO FRIEND LIKE A SISTER. 18th Thousand.
27. THE ANGEL OF FORGIVENESS. 17th Thousand.

THE NOVELS AND TALES OF

CHARLOTTE M. YONGE

THE HEIR OF REDCLYFFE. With Illustrations by KATE GREENAWAY.

HEARTSEASE ; or, the Brother's Wife. New Edition. With Illustrations by KATE GREENAWAY.

HOPES AND FEARS ; or, Scenes from the Life of a Spinster. With Illustrations by HERBERT GANDY.

DYNEVOR TERRACE ; or, the Clue of Life. With Illustrations by ADRIAN STOKES.

THE DAISY CHAIN ; or, Aspirations. A Family Chronicle With Illustrations by J. P. ATKINSON.

THE TRIAL : More Links of the Daisy Chain. With Illustrations by J. P. ATKINSON.

THE PILLARS OF THE HOUSE ; or, Under Wode, under Rode. Two Vols. With Illustrations by HERBERT GANDY.

THE YOUNG STEPMOTHER ; or, a Chronicle of Mistakes. With Illustrations by MARIAN HUXLEY.

THE CLEVER WOMAN OF THE FAMILY. With Illustrations by ADRIAN STOKES.

THE THREE BRIDES. With Illustrations by ADRIAN STOKES.

MY YOUNG ALCIDES : A Faded Photograph. With Illustrations by ADRIAN STOKES.

THE CAGED LION. With Illustrations by W. J. HENNESSY.

THE DOVE IN THE EAGLE'S NEST. With Illustrations by W. J. HENNESSY.

THE CHAPLET OF PEARLS ; or, the White and Black Ribaumont. With Illustrations by W. J. HENNESSY.

LADY HESTER ; or, Ursula's Narrative ; and THE DANVERS PAPERS. With Illustrations by JANE E. COOK.

MAGNUM BONUM ; or, Mother Carey's Brood. With Illustrations by W. J. HENNESSY.

LOVE AND LIFE : an Old Story in Eighteenth Century Costume. With Illustrations by W. J. HENNESSY.

UNKNOWN TO HISTORY. A Story of the Captivity of Mary of Scotland. With Illustrations by W. J. HENNESSY.

STRAY PEARLS. Memoirs of Margaret de Ribaumont, Viscountess of Bellaise. With Illustrations by W. J. HENNESSY.

THE NOVELS AND TALES OF

CHARLOTTE M. YONGE

THE ARMOURER'S 'PRENTICES. With Illustrations by W. J. HENNESSY.

SCENES AND CHARACTERS; or, Eighteen Months at Beechcroft. With Illustrations by W. J. HENNESSY.

CHANTRY HOUSE. With Illustrations by W. J. HENNESSY.

A MODERN TELEMACHUS. With Illustrations by W. J. HENNESSY.

BYWORDS. A collection of Tales new and old.

BEECHCROFT AT ROCKSTONE.

MORE BYWORDS.

A REPUTED CHANGELING; or, Three Seventh Years Two Centuries Ago.

THE LITTLE DUKE, RICHARD THE FEARLESS. With Illustrations.

THE LANCES OF LYNWOOD. With Illustrations by J. B.

THE PRINCE AND THE PAGE : A Story of the Last Crusade. With Illustrations by ADRIAN STOKES.

TWO PENNILESS PRINCESSES. With Illustrations by W. J. HENNESSY.

THAT STICK.

AN OLD WOMAN'S OUTLOOK IN A HAMPSHIRE VILLAGE.

GRISLY GRISELL; or, The Laidly Lady of Whitburn. A Tale of the Wars of the Roses.

HENRIETTA'S WISH. Second Edition.

THE LONG VACATION.

THE RELEASE ; or, Caroline's French Kindred.

THE PILGRIMAGE OF THE BEN BERIAH.

THE TWO GUARDIANS ; or, Home in this World. Second Edition.

COUNTESS KATE AND THE STOKESLEY SECRET.

MODERN BROODS ; or, Developments Unlooked for.

STROLLING PLAYERS : A Harmony of Contrasts. By C. M YONGE and C. R. COLERIDGE.

Works by Mrs. Craik

Olive: A Novel.   With Illustrations by G. Bowers.

Agatha's Husband: A Novel.   With Illustrations by
  Walter Crane.

The Head of the Family: A Novel.   With Illustrations
  by Walter Crane.

Two Marriages.

The Laurel Bush.

King Arthur: Not a Love Story.

About Money, and other Things.

Concerning Men, and other Papers.

Works by Mrs. Oliphant

Neighbours on the Green.

Kirsteen: the Story of a Scotch Family Seventy Years Ago.

A Beleaguered City: A Story of the Seen and the Unseen.

Hester: a Story of Contemporary Life.

He that Will Not when He May.

The Railway Man and his Children.

The Marriage of Elinor.

Sir Tom.

The Heir-Presumptive and the Heir-Apparent.

A Country Gentleman and his Family.

A Son of the Soil.

The Second Son.

The Wizard's Son: A Novel.

Lady William.

Young Musgrave.

The Works of Dean Farrar

SEEKERS AFTER GOD.   The Lives of Seneca, Epictetus, and Marcus Aurelius.

ETERNAL HOPE.   Sermons preached in Westminster Abbey.

THE FALL OF MAN : and other Sermons.

THE WITNESS OF HISTORY TO CHRIST.

THE SILENCE AND VOICES OF GOD, with other Sermons.

"IN THE DAYS OF THY YOUTH."   Sermons on Practical Subjects.

SAINTLY WORKERS.   Five Lenten Lectures.

EPHPHATHA ; or, the Amelioration of the World.

MERCY AND JUDGMENT : a few last words on Christian Eschatology.

SERMONS & ADDRESSES DELIVERED IN AMERICA.

THE WORKS OF

Frederick Denison Maurice

SERMONS PREACHED IN LINCOLN'S INN CHAPEL. In six vols.

SERMONS PREACHED IN COUNTRY CHURCHES.

CHRISTMAS DAY : and other Sermons.

THEOLOGICAL ESSAYS.

THE PROPHETS AND KINGS OF THE OLD TESTAMENT.

THE PATRIARCHS AND LAWGIVERS OF THE OLD TESTAMENT.

THE GOSPEL OF THE KINGDOM OF HEAVEN.

THE GOSPEL OF ST. JOHN.

THE EPISTLES OF ST. JOHN.

THE FRIENDSHIP OF BOOKS : and other Lectures.

THE PRAYER BOOK AND THE LORD'S PRAYER.

THE DOCTRINE OF SACRIFICE.   Deduced from the Scriptures.

THE ACTS OF THE APOSTLES.

THE KINGDOM OF CHRIST ; or, Hints to a Quaker respecting the Principles, Constitution, and Ordinances of the Catholic Church.   2 vols.

By J. H. SHORTHOUSE

JOHN INGLESANT: A Romance.

SIR PERCIVAL: a Story of the Past and of the Present.

THE LITTLE SCHOOLMASTER MARK.

THE COUNTESS EVE.

A TEACHER OF THE VIOLIN.

BLANCHE, LADY FALAISE.

By GERTRUDE ATHERTON

THE CONQUEROR.

A DAUGHTER OF THE VINE.

THE CALIFORNIANS.

By HUGH CONWAY

A FAMILY AFFAIR.

By W. CLARK RUSSELL

MAROONED.

By ANNIE KEARY

A YORK AND A LANCASTER ROSE.

CASTLE DALY: the Story of an Irish Home thirty years ago.

JANET'S HOME. | OLDBURY.

A DOUBTING HEART.

THE NATIONS AROUND ISRAEL.

By THOMAS HUGHES

TOM BROWN'S SCHOOLDAYS.

TOM BROWN AT OXFORD.

THE SCOURING OF THE WHITE HORSE.

ALFRED THE GREAT.

By ARCHIBALD FORBES

BARRACKS, BIVOUACS, AND BATTLES.

SOUVENIRS OF SOME CONTINENTS.

By MONTAGU WILLIAMS

LEAVES OF A LIFE. | LATER LEAVES.

ROUND LONDON.

By E. WERNER

FICKLE FORTUNE.

By W. E. NORRIS

THIRLBY HALL.

A BACHELOR'S BLUNDER.

The Works of SHAKESPEARE

VICTORIA EDITION. In Three Volumes.

Vol. I. COMEDIES. Vol. II. HISTORIES. Vol. III. TRAGEDIES.

UNIFORM EDITION OF THE
NOVELS OF CHARLES LEVER

With all the Original Illustrations.

1. HARRY LORREQUER. Illustrated by PHIZ.
2. CHARLES O'MALLEY. Illustrated by PHIZ.
3. JACK HINTON THE GUARDSMAN. Illustrated by PHIZ.
4. TOM BURKE OF OURS. Illustrated by PHIZ.
5. ARTHUR O'LEARY. Illustrated by G. CRUIKSHANK.
6. LORD KILGOBBIN. Illustrated by LUKE FILDES.

By W. WARDE FOWLER

A YEAR WITH THE BIRDS. Illustrated.

TALES OF THE BIRDS. Illustrated.

MORE TALES OF THE BIRDS. Illustrated.

SUMMER STUDIES OF BIRDS AND BOOKS.

By FRANK BUCKLAND

CURIOSITIES OF NATURAL HISTORY. Illustrated. In four volumes :

FIRST SERIES—Rats, Serpents, Fishes, Frogs, Monkeys, etc.

SECOND SERIES—Fossils, Bears, Wolves, Cats, Eagles, Hedgehogs, Eels, Herrings, Whales.

THIRD SERIES—Wild Ducks, Fishing, Lions, Tigers, Foxes, Porpoises.

FOURTH SERIES—Giants, Mummies, Mermaids, Wonderful People, Salmon, etc.

Works by Various Authors

Hogan, M.P.
Flitters, Tatters, and the Counsellor
The New Antigone
Memories of Father Healy
CANON ATKINSON.—The Last of the Giant Killers
·—— Playhours and Half-Holidays; or, further Experiences of Two Schoolboys
SIR S. BAKER.—True Tales for my Grandsons
R. H. BARHAM.—The Ingoldsby Legends
REV. R. H. D. BARHAM.—Life of Theodore Hook
BLENNERHASSET AND SLEEMAN.—Adventures in Mashonaland
LANOE FALCONER.—Cecilia de Noël
W. FORBES-MITCHELL.—Reminiscences of the Great Mutiny
REV. J. GILMORE.—Storm Warriors
MARY LINSKILL.—Tales of the North Riding
S. R. LYSAGHT.—The Marplot
—— One of the Grenvilles
M. M'LENNAN.—Muckle Jock, and other Stories
LUCAS MALET.—Mrs. Lorimer
G. MASSON.—A Compendious Dictionary of the French Language
MAJOR GAMBIER PARRY.—The Story of Dick
E. C. PRICE.—In the Lion's Mouth
LORD REDESDALE.—Tales of Old Japan
W. C. RHOADES.—John Trevennick
MARCHESA THEODOLI.—Under Pressure
ANTHONY TROLLOPE.—The Three Clerks
CHARLES WHITEHEAD.—Richard Savage

ENGLISH
MEN OF LETTERS
EDITED BY JOHN MORLEY.

Arranged in 13 Volumes, each containing the Lives of three Authors.

I. **Chaucer.** By Dr. A. W. WARD. **Spenser.** By Dean CHURCH. **Dryden.** By Prof. SAINTSBURY.

II. **Milton.** By MARK PATTISON. **Goldsmith.** By W. BLACK. **Cowper.** By GOLDWIN SMITH.

III. **Byron.** By Professor NICHOL. **Shelley.** By J. A. SYMONDS. **Keats.** By SIDNEY COLVIN.

IV. **Wordsworth.** By F. W. H. MYERS. **Southey.** By Prof. DOWDEN. **Landor.** By SIDNEY COLVIN.

V. **Charles Lamb.** By Canon AINGER. **Addison.** By W. J. COURTHOPE. **Swift.** By Sir LESLIE STEPHEN, K.C.B.

VI. **Scott.** By R. H. HUTTON. **Burns.** By Principal SHAIRP. **Coleridge.** By H. D. TRAILL.

VII. **Hume.** By Prof. HUXLEY, F.R.S. **Locke.** By THOS. FOWLER. **Burke.** By JOHN MORLEY.

VIII. **Defoe.** By W. MINTO. **Sterne.** By H. D. TRAILL. **Hawthorne.** By HENRY JAMES.

IX. **Fielding.** By AUSTIN DOBSON. **Thackeray.** By ANTHONY TROLLOPE. **Dickens.** By Dr. A. W. WARD.

X. **Gibbon.** By J. C. MORISON. **Carlyle.** By Professor NICHOL. **Macaulay.** By J. C. MORISON.

XI. **Sydney.** By J. A. SYMONDS. **De Quincey.** By Prof. MASSON. **Sheridan.** By Mrs. OLIPHANT.

XII. **Pope.** By Sir LESLIE STEPHEN, K.C.B. **Johnson.** By Sir LESLIE STEPHEN, K.C.B. **Gray.** By EDMUND GOSSE.

XIII. **Bacon.** By Dean CHURCH. **Bunyan.** By J. A. FROUDE. **Bentley.** By Sir RICHARD JEBB.

THE GLOBE LIBRARY

Crown 8vo. 3s. 6d. each.

The volumes marked with an asterisk (*) are also issued in limp leather, with full gilt back and gilt edges. 5s. net each.

*Boswell's Life of Johnson. With an Introduction by MOWBRAY MORRIS.

*Burns's Complete Works. Edited from the best Printed and MS. Authorities, with Memoir and Glossarial Index. By A. SMITH.

*The Works of Geoffrey Chaucer. Edited by ALFRED W. POLLARD, H. F. HEATH, M. H. LIDDELL, and W. S. McCORMICK.

*Cowper's Poetical Works. Edited, with Biographical Introduction and Notes by W. BENHAM, B.D.

Robinson Crusoe. Edited after the original Edition, with a Biographical Introduction by HENRY KINGSLEY, F.R.G.S.

*Dryden's Poetical Works. Edited, with a Memoir, Revised Texts, and Notes, by W. D. CHRISTIE, M.A.

*The Diary of John Evelyn. With an Introduction and Notes by AUSTIN DOBSON, Hon. LL.D. Edin.

Froissart's Chronicles. Translated by Lord BERNERS. Edited by G. C. MACAULAY, M.A.

*Goldsmith's Miscellaneous Works. With Biographical Introduction by Professor MASSON.

Horace. Rendered into English Prose, with Introduction, Running Analysis, Notes, and Index. By J. LONSDALE, M.A., and S. LEE, M.A.

*The Poetical Works of John Keats. Edited, with Introduction and Notes, by WILLIAM T. ARNOLD.

Morte Darthur. The Book of King Arthur, and of his Noble Knights of the Round Table. The Original Edition of Caxton, revised for modern use. With Introduction, Notes, and Glossary. By Sir E. STRACHEY. [by Professor MASSON.

*Milton's Poetical Works. Edited, with Introduction,

*The Diary of Samuel Pepys. With an Introduction and Notes by G. GREGORY SMITH.

*Pope's Poetical Works. Edited, with Notes and Introductory Memoir, by Dr. A. W. WARD.

*Sir Walter Scott's Poetical Works. Edited, with Biographical and Critical Memoir, by Prof. F. T. PALGRAVE. With Introduction and Notes.

*Shakespeare's Complete Works. Edited by W. G. CLARK, M.A., and W. ALDIS WRIGHT, M.A. With Glossary.

*Spenser's Complete Works. Edited from the Original Editions and Manuscripts, with Glossary, by R. MORRIS, and a Memoir by J. W. HALES, M.A. [edges. 4s. 6d.]

*Tennyson's Poetical Works. [Also in extra cloth, gilt

Virgil. Rendered into English Prose, with Introductions, Notes Analysis, and Index. By J. LONSDALE, M.A., and S. LEE, M.A.

ILLUSTRATED
STANDARD NOVELS

Crown 8vo. Cloth Elegant, gilt edges (Peacock Edition).
3s. 6d. each.

Also issued in ornamental cloth binding. 2s. 6d. each.

By JANE AUSTEN

With Introductions by AUSTIN DOBSON, *and Illustrations by*
HUGH THOMSON *and* C. E. BROCK.

PRIDE AND PREJUDICE.
SENSE AND SENSIBILITY.
EMMA.

MANSFIELD PARK.
NORTHANGER ABBEY,
AND PERSUASION.

By J. FENIMORE COOPER

With Illustrations by C. E. BROCK *and* H. M. BROCK.

THE LAST OF THE MOHICANS. With a General Introduction by Mowbray Morris.

THE DEERSLAYER.
THE PATHFINDER.

THE PIONEERS.
THE PRAIRIE.

By MARIA EDGEWORTH

With Introductions by ANNE THACKERAY RITCHIE, *and Illustrations by* CHRIS HAMMOND *and* CARL SCHLOESSER.

ORMOND.
CASTLE RACKRENT, AND
THE ABSENTEE.
POPULAR TALES.

HELEN.
BELINDA.
PARENT'S ASSISTANT.

By CAPTAIN MARRYAT

With Introductions by DAVID HANNAY, *and Illustrations by*
H. M. BROCK, J. AYTON SYMINGTON, FRED PEGRAM, F. H.
TOWNSEND, H. R. MILLAR, *and* E. J. SULLIVAN.

JAPHET IN SEARCH OF
A FATHER.

JACOB FAITHFUL.
PETER SIMPLE.

ILLUSTRATED
STANDARD NOVELS
By CAPTAIN MARRYAT—*continued.*

MIDSHIPMAN EASY.	THE PIRATE, AND THE
THE KING'S OWN.	THREE CUTTERS.
THE PHANTOM SHIP.	MASTERMAN READY.
SNARLEY-YOW.	FRANK MILDMAY.
POOR JACK.	NEWTON FORSTER.

By THOMAS LOVE PEACOCK

With Introductions by GEORGE SAINTSBURY, *and Illustrations by* H. R. MILLAR *and* F. H. TOWNSEND.

HEADLONG HALL, AND	GRYLL GRANGE.
NIGHTMARE ABBEY.	MELINCOURT.
MAID MARIAN, AND	MISFORTUNES OF ELPHIN
CROTCHET CASTLE.	AND RHODODAPHNE.

BY VARIOUS AUTHORS

WESTWARD HO! By CHARLES KINGSLEY. Illustrated by C. E. Brock.

HANDY ANDY. By SAMUEL LOVER. Illustrated by H. M. Brock. With Introduction by Charles Whibley.

TOM CRINGLE'S LOG. By MICHAEL SCOTT. Illustrated by J. Ayton Symington. With Introduction by Mowbray Morris.

ANNALS OF THE PARISH. By JOHN GALT. Illustrated By C. E. Brock. With Introduction by Alfred Ainger.

SYBIL, OR THE TWO NATIONS, ETC. By BENJAMIN DISRAELI. Illustrated by F. Pegram. With Introduction by H. D. Traill.

LAVENGRO. By GEORGE BORROW. Illustrated by E. J. Sullivan. With Introduction by Augustine Birrell, K.C.

ADVENTURES OF HAJJI BABA OF ISPAHAN. By JAMES MORIER. Illustrated by H. R. Millar. With Introduction by Lord Curzon.

THE NEW CRANFORD SERIES

Crown 8vo, Cloth Elegant, Gilt Edges, 3s. 6d. per volume.

Cranford. By Mrs. GASKELL. With Preface by Anne
Thackeray Ritchie and 100 Illustrations by Hugh Thomson.

The Vicar of Wakefield. With 182 Illustrations by
Hugh Thomson, and Preface by Austin Dobson.

Our Village. By MARY RUSSELL MITFORD. Introduction
by Anne Thackeray Ritchie, and 100 Illustrations by Hugh Thomson.

Gulliver's Travels. With Introduction by Sir Henry
Craik, K.C.B., and 100 Illustrations by C. E. Brock.

The Humorous Poems of Thomas Hood. With
Preface by Alfred Ainger, and 130 Illustrations by C. E. Brock.

Sheridan's The School for Scandal and The Rivals.
Illustrated by E. J. Sullivan. With Introduction by A. Birrell.

Household Stories. By the Brothers GRIMM. Translated
by Lucy Crane. With Pictures by Walter Crane.

Reynard the Fox. Edited by J. JACOBS. With Illustrations by W. Frank Calderon.

Coaching Days and Coaching Ways. By W. OUTRAM
TRISTRAM. With Illustrations by H. Railton and Hugh Thomson.

Coridon's Song; and other Verses. With Introduction by
Austin Dobson and Illustrations by Hugh Thomson.

The Fables of Æsop. Selected by JOSEPH JACOBS. Illustrated by R. Heighway.

Old Christmas. By WASHINGTON IRVING. With Illustrations by R. Caldecott.

Bracebridge Hall. With Illustrations by R. CALDECOTT.

Rip Van Winkle and the Legend of Sleepy Hollow.
With 50 Illustrations and a Preface by George H. Boughton, A.R.A.

The Alhambra. With Illustrations by J. Pennell and
Introduction by E. R. Pennell.

MACMILLAN & CO., LTD., LONDON.

J. PALMER, PRINTER, CAMBRIDGE.   20.8.10